From: Erin Thatcher
To: Samantha Tyler; Tess Norton
Subject: Men To Do

Whose idea was it for the reading group to spend a month on erotica? Did we need another reminder of the sad state of our sex lives?

Which brings me to my subject line: Men to do before saying "I do!" I'm talking about the type of man no girl in her right mind would settle down with. But wouldn't it be great to do it all wrong before we find Mr. Right?

What do you think? Couldn't we use an uncomplicated sexfest? No guilt, no worries. Why let men corner the market on fun when we girls have the same urges and needs?

Me, I'm taking The Scary Guy. Yes. The one I told you about. The one living upstairs.

Erin

Erin hit Send and shut down her e-mail. It was crazy to be thinking about her dark, mysteriously sexy neighbor in the condo above hers. For all she knew, he could be a thug of the highest order. But she couldn't stop the nightly fantasy of his hands on her body, cupping her breasts, his touch setting her skin on fire. Erin smiled to herself. She knew what she had to do....

Dear Reader,

Where do you get your ideas?

I don't know a single author who hasn't been asked that
question. Well, in this case the answer is easy. The concept of
finding a "Man To Do Before Saying 'I Do!'" came straight from
the pages of a women's magazine. When I read the article, I was
inspired—the perfect concept for Blaze. And sharing the fun
with Isabel Sharpe and Jo Leigh made perfect sense, as you'll
see when you read their upcoming stories *A Taste of Fantasy*
and *A Dash of Temptation.*

For my own story, I couldn't resist exploring a hero who had
created his own identity—literally—the same way he creates the
identities of the fictional characters about whom he writes. And
the best part was that I got to do all the creating, of his characters
as well as mine. I also felt myself drawn to a heroine grounded in
family, but not familial duty. How would she deal with a hero
who shared none of her experiences yet often knew her better
than she knew herself? Oh, yes. I love writing!

I hope you enjoy *The Sweetest Taboo* and that you'll visit me
at www.alisonkent.com as well as www.eHarlequin.com and
let me know what you think about the story and the idea of
MEN TO DO.

Alison Kent

P.S. Check out more on MEN TO DO at www.mentodo.com.

Books by Alison Kent

HARLEQUIN BLAZE
24—ALL TIED UP
32—NO STRINGS ATTACHED
40—BOUND TO HAPPEN

HARLEQUIN TEMPTATION
741—THE BADGE AND THE BABY
750—FOUR MEN & A LADY

THE SWEETEST TABOO

Alison Kent

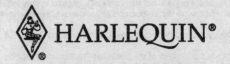

TORONTO • NEW YORK • LONDON
AMSTERDAM • PARIS • SYDNEY • HAMBURG
STOCKHOLM • ATHENS • TOKYO • MILAN • MADRID
PRAGUE • WARSAW • BUDAPEST • AUCKLAND

To Muna Shehadi Sill and Jolie Kramer—
over 200,000 words written and men remain a mystery!
Ain't it grand!

This one is for the man to whom I said, "I do."
I love you, Walt.

ISBN 0-373-79072-4

THE SWEETEST TABOO

1

HE WAS PLAYING THE blues again.

The melancholy and menacing low-down sounds wound their way through her bedroom's open window, conjuring wild and reckless images in her wandering mind. Feet tucked beneath her in the bedroom's overstuffed reading chair, Erin Thatcher placed the open copy of Anaïs Nin's *Little Birds* facedown on the quilted throw covering her lap.

With her hands resting on the chair's padded arms, her head sinking into the cushioned back, she closed her eyes and listened. The rhythm worked the magic she'd come to expect from the sultry sounds, arousing the parts of her body the erotica had wickedly stirred to life.

She wanted to indulge in the sensations, to let the music take her places she hadn't visited in far too long, to offer her experiences rich with the sensual encounters and adventures her reading of late reminded her she was missing.

The guitar strings stroked velvet fingers the length of her neck, caressing her skin from her chin to the hollow of her throat. The singer's voice filled her ears with dirty words and sweet nothings, whispered suggestions of bodies belonging together and loving long into the night. Hearing so much in the music said a lot about the silence in her life.

Oh, the crowd at Paddington's On Main was noisy enough, but the downtown Houston, Texas, wine and tobacco bar was her career. A career she loved. A career she'd been destined for since first visiting the UK with her parents, standing but knee-high to her Granddad Rory behind the counter in his quayside pub deep in Devon's lush countryside.

But it was not a career that met her personal needs and desires. Neither her regular customers nor her co-workers—no matter how much she enjoyed the interaction with both—touched that part of her soul that knew there was more to life than the endless hours she devoted to work.

Hours she knew Rory would never have wanted her to spend, but how could she do any less? Paddington's was her legacy from the granddad she'd already lost. And she would do everything in her power to keep the bar afloat.

After all the years he'd devoted to her upbringing, the sacrifices he'd made on her behalf, the remorse of letting him down would be too much to bear. She couldn't chance losing his dream, not when she wasn't certain she'd ever recover from losing him.

Right now, however, at this moment, the one thing of which she was selfishly feeling the loss, the one thing her life was missing above all else, was intimacy of the most basic sort. One man and one woman. Simple and to the point.

She had friends galore, both here in town and in cyberspace. It was, in fact, the literary erotica her on-line reading group had chosen to read this month that had her so restless, furthering her discontent with this one part of her life—the only part of her life—in which she felt lacking.

And now he was playing the blues again.

She wanted to know who *he* was.

He'd lived in the loft above hers since, several months before, she'd moved into the newly-converted, one-hundred-year-old hotel on the edge of Houston's theater district.

They crossed paths in the mail room, the tomblike space too small for the two of them and the mutual attraction which hovered like a heavy cloud of bone-soaking rain.

They ran into one another in the garage. His classic black GTO lurked at the end of the row where she parked her Toyota Camry, a darkly menacing presence lying in wait.

They passed each other coming in and out of the elevator on the ground floor. Neither gave the other wide berth. Instead, each seemed to have the need to test unspoken limits, to brush clothing, to breathe the same air, to measure the fit of bodies…

Enough already!

Pushing her way up out of the chair and dragging the quilt behind her, Erin padded across the hardwood floor of her bedroom, her socks slip-sliding on the smoothly grained surface. She pulled back the simple muslin panel along the antique brass rod and climbed into the window seat, tugging her sleep shirt over her updrawn knees and cocooning herself in the warm cotton knit and the quilt.

It was dark here, away from the single lamp she'd left on for reading. Here in the very corner of her room, far from the hallway door and the rest of the pitch-black loft, six stories above the ground. It was dark and it was cold and the clock was ticking its way toward 3:00 a.m.

But from here she could hear the muted noises of the traffic below, watch the brake lights and blinkers of the cars leaving the city's nightlife behind. And she could smell the smoke curling from the end of the cigar he inevitably smoked while the blues made love to the night.

She could so easily picture him, leaning on the window ledge, elbows bracing his weight, hand holding the dangling cigar, thumb flicking ashes from the end. He always wore dark colors—navy, burgundy, black and pine. Tonight, unseasonably cool for early October, her imagination dressed him in a crew-neck cashmere sweater.

He'd wear it loose, rather than tucking it into his jeans. The hem would bunch loosely around his hips, inviting her hands to explore the tempting skin beneath. He'd have on expensive black leather boots and his hair, cut short only on the sides and the back, left overly, rebelliously long on top, would fall over his forehead, to his darkly slashed brows and starburst lashes, skimming eyes an incongruously light shade of green.

Why she was playing fantasy dress-up, she had no idea. Except, perhaps, for the possibility that she'd never been easily intimidated. And that single personality quirk inspired her to figure out why the idea of actually sharing the building's tiny, slow-moving elevator with the man set her temperature on the same upward climb.

Or why she checked his parking space each time she pulled into hers, the skin on the back of her neck prickling hot at the thought of being caught alone with him in the ominously gloomy garage. Or why the click of his key in his mailbox, echoing in the small basement, resounded through her body like a shot to the heart.

Okay. Now she was exaggerating. He had to have at least one or two redeeming qualities or he'd wouldn't be living where he lived. She knew exactly the type of invasive background checks mortgage companies and tenant associations put a body through…unless that body had paid cash, another possibility that had occurred to her as the man hadn't kept any sort of regular hours since she'd known him.

Except she didn't know him. And so she shouldn't be noticing his comings and goings.

She was noticing both and far more. Things that a sane and practical woman would have the sense to ignore. Or at least to pass off as surface attraction. Shoulders accentuated beneath dark fabric. Legs confident in their long, rangy stride. Hands large enough and strong enough to palm a basketball. Or a woman's throat.

Erin shuddered. She had to be at least six degrees of sick to find his formidable aura intriguing. Her sex drive might be steering her thought processes but she'd be damned before her brain forgot how to apply the brakes. Brooding good looks did not serious boink material make.

For all she knew, he could be a thug of the highest order. The possibility of bodies beneath the floorboards wasn't much of a concern considering he lived on the seventh floor and she lived underneath on the sixth. Trafficking in narcotics or currency or plutonium, however, wasn't so easily ruled out.

Okay. Now she was borrowing libelous trouble. But wasn't trouble par for the Erin Thatcher course. If math and memory served her correctly, curiosity had already snatched away at least four of her nine lives.

Those were relationships, Erin. That's not what we're talking about here.

What was she talking about? Sex with an improper stranger? Ha! If *that* wouldn't make a perfect *Cosmo* headline, she didn't know what would. *Wait a minute.* A flash of memory flickered over her head and ruined the moody ambience. Throwing off the quilt, the music and her imagination, she jumped to her feet, sock-shushing her way back across the room. Hadn't she just seen another article…

She flopped belly first onto her bed, flipping through the pages of the magazine she'd picked up earlier today. The magazine with the article that had caught her eye. The article about finding a Man To Do before saying, "I do!" Not that she planned to say any such thing any time soon.

But she did like the "go for it" sentiment behind the article. How cool it would be to ignore practicalities. To make entertaining conquests. To collect raunchy stories to share with her girlfriends. Not to mention having a hell of a lot of healthy naked fun.

And, thinking further, she knew two other single and sexually frustrated females who could benefit from a little living it up with a scandalously inappropriate man. Tess and Samantha both deserved to take a tumble with their own highly desirable Mr. Wrong.

Along with Erin, both women belonged to Eve's Apple, an online reading group devoted to literary temptation, from sensory enticement to intellectual appeal to the most basic and provocative exploration of adventurous sex.

Sex that not a one of the three of them were having.

Erin reached across to her bedside table where she'd left her laptop last night after spending too many hours in her office working on the budget for Paddington's upcoming anniversary celebration.

Settling back into the pillows propped against her headboard, she began composing an e-mail that she knew would raise at least one eyebrow in both Chicago and New York City.

From: Erin Thatcher
Sent: Wednesday
To: Samantha Tyler; Tess Norton
Subject: Magazine Article on Doing Men

Considering the reading group's recent fixation with literary erotica, I decided a themed and attention-grabbing subject line appropriate. ::snort::

Speaking of the group (and don't get me wrong—I adore the diversity of the Eve's Apple membership), whose idea was it *anyway* to spend an entire month reading Anaïs Nin? Did we need another reminder of the sad state of our sex lives? I can't believe I've let myself become so consumed with work, especially when Rory taught me better. And now with this do-or-die anniversary celebration for Paddington's...

Figures, doesn't it? The one time I could use a man to help me shag off a bit of this frustration I don't have one. Which brings me back to my subject line.

Here, girls, we have a veritable smorgasbord of unsuitable men. ("Rascals, rakes and rapscallions!") The type of man no girl in her right mind would settle down with but, hey, we're talking about a fling. At least *I'm* talking about a fling.

The article's title says it all: *Men To Do Before Saying, "I do!"* We know we'll eventually do the right thing with the right guy, but wouldn't it be great to do it all wrong first? With no guilt and no worries?

What do you think? Samantha? With all you're going through? Couldn't you use an uncomplicated sex fest? And, Tess. One of the men mentioned is The Playboy. How conveniently perfect, don't you think? <wink>

Why let men corner the market on fun when we girls have the same urges and needs? We can't possibly get into any trouble if we do this with our eyes wide open, right? Me, I'm taking The Scary Guy. Yes. The one I told you about. The one living upstairs.

I know, I know. You're both wondering if I've lost my mind. But you know I've never been one to jump out of my skin and these days its happening round the clock. Even now. I have goose bumps like you can't imagine. My bedroom window's open and I can hear his music and I can smell his cigar and I want to feel his hands.

I'm not sure how to pull this off since every time I see the man I forget how to put two words together. How do you tell a guy you don't even know that he's just won the bloomin' sex lottery? Love you both!

Erin scanned the e-mail for typos then hit Send before changing her mind. She shut down the system and returned her laptop to the bedside table, switching off the lamp and snuggling into down feathers and plush Egyptian cotton. She was ridiculously hedonistic when it came to the haven of her bed. And a haven was exactly what it was.

This one room was her personal sanctuary. She refused to bring business through the doorway, keeping Paddington's and all it entailed to her home office or the larger office she kept at the bar. This room was for dreaming, for reading, for letting her imagination run wild and indulging when she had a partner with whom to share her fantasies.

She'd meant what she'd said in her e-mail to Samantha and Tess. A relationship would come in good time for all of them. But this wasn't Erin's time. She had no ticking biological clock, no urge to hyphenate her last name, no desire to redecorate the red and gold harem of her bathroom with his and hers monogrammed towels.

Right now her focus had to be on Paddington's end-of-month anniversary celebration.

The bar had belonged to the grandfather who'd taken her in at the age of eleven, after a trip to the Serengeti had taken her parents and left her in Rory Thatcher's capable hands. He'd gone so far as to move from England to the U.S., wanting her to be comfortable growing up in the country she called home.

Rory had taught her not to pour all her energy into work but to save the best of everything she had for living. For the past year, she hadn't lived much at all. She'd worked her fanny off seeing to his dream of keeping Paddington's alive in the States after giving up the English pub that had been his life long before Erin had been born.

When he'd left this world three years ago, he'd only been fifty-seven, too bloody young to die. He'd lived a full and blessed life, right up to that very last minute. And Erin wanted to live the same. To grab the brass ring. To go for the gusto. To do all the things advertising guaranteed would make life the best it could be.

She smiled softly to herself as she began to drift off to sleep. She'd left her window open. Though the breeze was a little bit chilly, Erin remained warm, burrowed down in her bed and wrapped up in her imagination. The heat of the music blew warm liquid notes over her skin. The heated aroma of the richly smooth cigar teased her nostrils.

But it was the heat of The Scary Guy's hands as she imagined them roaming beneath her bedcovers and over her body, his fingertips tap-dancing the length of her breastbone, his widespread palm cupping the curve of her waist, his thumb tugging at the elastic edge of her string bikinis, that set her on fire.

Her hands became his hands, her fingers his fingers, the pleasure she found enhanced by sharing his taste in music and the imagined smoke of his fine cigar. Sensation became unbearable. Her skin burned and sizzled and sparked. Dampness grew, seeping and spreading from her sex to her thighs.

And her touch, his touch, swept upward to the source, stroking along either side of the tight knot of nerves where sensation centered, slipping through the slickness he drew from her body, fingering the soft pillow of her inner core where the pleasure of waiting bordered on pain.

When she finally came, she reached for the edge with abandon, crying out her release with a breathless catch, a sob of exquisite satisfaction that wanted to know his name. Replete, exhausted and tingling still, she turned to her side and curled her body around the lingering high.

It was only then, when the night closed around her

and the silence set in, that she realized the music had stopped. Erin held her breath and, swore above the beat of her heart, she heard the beat of his.

Chapter 2

He watched her from the shadows fringing his world. Shadows that protected him from prying minds, prying eyes. Her mind, her eyes, her certainty that she held his salvation in the palm of her hand.

She was innocence embodied. Chaste and uncorrupt. And he was going to take her down, drag her to the gutter, show her the reality of the life he called hell.

She thought she knew him. He'd seen the brash confidence in her eyes. And he'd seen more. Flickers of quick-witted fear. A switchblade-sharp awareness. Vigilance. Watchfulness. She knew the truth. That once he got his hands on her she wouldn't want him to let her go.

He was certain that was the reason she hovered on the edge of his existence. He wondered how long caution would keep her curiosity bound. If her strength of character could withstand the destruction of her faith in mankind. In him. In herself.

Raleigh Slater choked back the crazed laughter eating at his throat. She wasn't the first. There had been others. Women who'd driven to the brink of his twilight, headlights cutting through the fog that concealed his dead end. He wasn't giving this one time to shift into reverse. Not until he'd fed her a taste of what she'd driven this far to find.

*She'd never even know. She'd swear she'd been
dreaming. That what she'd felt moving over her
body while she slept had been nothing but the
workings of her mind. Only Raleigh would know
the reality of his possession. That what she'd
thought she'd imagined, in truth, she had lived.*

Sebastian Gallo saved the document and shut down
his notebook computer. He'd had enough. Deadline or
no deadline, he'd had enough. He needed a beer. He
needed several. But he'd waited too long to go out.

The bars were closed for the night and now he'd
have to put off until tomorrow what he needed to do
today—to find a dark corner at Paddington's On Main
and watch Erin Thatcher pretend he didn't make her
sweat.

He needed to feel that edge, that cutting, biting
awareness that he'd learned back when he was living
on the streets and honed during his years in lockup. It
was what kept him alive and kept him going. Fueled
his high-performance artistry. Jump-started the creative
bitch of a muse currently giving him hell.

A hell separate from her usual attempts at rewriting
every word he wrote. No, this hell was harsh and demanding, a foot-stomping insistence that he set aside
what she considered an unhealthy concentration on the
macabre to write the book aching to break free from
his heart. That's when he had to remind her that he
didn't have a heart—the very reason he and Raleigh
Slater got along so well.

Yep, he and Raleigh had more than a thing or two
in common, but it was this latest obsession with a mysterious woman that was going to cause the both of them
more than a man's fair share of trouble. Raleigh's prob-

lem was easily taken care of. Backspace. Delete. And his fictional world was set dead to rights.

The disruption to Sebastian's well-ordered life required more than fancy finger work. He needed sleep but was afraid his mental gears were wound too tightly to shut down. The cigar hadn't helped.

And the music, the blues, usually soothing in a twisted sort of way, had done nothing but speed up the beat of his heart, pumping blood into parts of his body that remained on edge no matter the intensity of his physical workouts. Or the long hot showers that followed.

He swore he'd heard her voice. After the music had stopped and before he'd put out the cigar and moved away from the window to reread the pages he'd written. The sound had crashed around him like lightning. White-hot electric jolts had nearly taken him out of his skin.

Now, minutes later, he wasn't sure if what he'd heard had been all in his head, a sound from the city street below, or the cry of a woman in the throes of pure bliss.

Sebastian laughed under his breath, muttering a curse that had nothing to do with the woman living below him and everything to do with his obsession instead. He shucked off his sweater, scratched the ball of black wool over his chest before tossing it to the floor at the foot of his bed where it skidded up against the clothes he'd worn yesterday and the day before. One of these days he'd have to find time for laundry. And, he cringed, for the dishes in the kitchen sink.

His boots came next, the metal buckles hitting the hardwood floor with a sharp clatter. He released the button fly of his jeans and headed for the shower, stopping only to scratch Redrum behind the ears. The black cat lay curled in a ball of sleep and fur on top of the room's highboy dresser.

At Sebastian's touch, she stretched, yawned and returned to ignoring him which she did so well. He chuckled before leaning down and, in a voice husky and rough from rarely speaking to anyone other than his agent or the cat, purred into her ear.

"Yes, cat. You do your job well." A job that entailed nothing more than reminding him of his invisibility, the condition once a hardship but now a valued commodity.

Redrum's cold shoulder was easy to laugh off without causing Sebastian any grief. Or distracting his creative muse as Erin Thatcher had managed to do. It was all Sebastian's fault that she affected him any way at all. His obsession had actually taken him to the mailroom where he'd discovered her name. She had no idea she'd picked up a stalker, though he, at least, did his stalking in his mind.

Raleigh Slater stalked women between the pages of the *New York Times* bestselling horror novels Sebastian wrote under the Ryder Falco pseudonym. But in Sebastian's world, a solitary existence of his own making, an isolation nothing like the years he'd spent forcibly confined by the courts in juvenile hall, the only real stalking was done by Redrum.

The black cat did her damndest to sneak up on the pigeons that fluttered on and off the loft's windowsill. Rats with wings, to Redrum's way of seeing things. To Sebastian's, too.

Reaching the bathroom enclosure—the dressing area and separate custom-designed shower space nearly half the size of his bedroom—he shucked off his jeans and boxer briefs, scratching all the body parts needing scratching before stepping beneath the blistering spray that rained down from three separate shower heads on three separate walls.

For the past sixteen years, since his release at age eighteen from the lockup where he'd spent his formative years, Sebastian had considered his showers as much about relaxation and clearing his mind as about cleaning his body. When he'd finally convinced himself he could deal with permanence, he'd made sure to allow the money and the room for the bathroom he needed to accomplish those goals.

For too many years he'd been allowed but a fifteen-minute shower four times a week, a shower shared with other boys considered a threat to society or to self. At least one out of each week's four soap-and-self-defense sessions resulted in a fight, a near riot…or worse. Sebastian had managed to escape unscathed and undetected.

Because the day he'd been taken from the street where he'd lived alone since the scrappy age of eleven, he'd made a promise to himself, a promise that he would never look to another human being for security or sustenance or support.

He chuckled to himself, wondering if he'd really been eleven at the time he'd been picked up by social services. Or if he'd been closer to twelve. He'd changed his age with the changes to his body, finally deciding on sixteen when his voice dropped and his balls dropped and the hair on his face began to grow as thick as that in his crotch.

He hadn't given a damn what age the courts declared him. He'd made up his own mind—relying on remembered images of candles and crushed cupcakes and little toy trucks—and counted forward.

Even now he had no idea how old he really was. All those ages and dates were as much a part of his imagination as Raleigh Slater.

Or as much as the fictional fantasies he wove of Erin Thatcher.

Sebastian reached for the bar of soap and ran it over his chest and armpits, working up a lather before stepping back beneath the spray to rinse. He kept his eyes closed, the hazy fog so thick he couldn't see much of anything. He could barely even breathe. His skin burned from the stinging heat of the water. And from the mental picture of Erin. A picture of her sharing the heat and the steam. A steam that intensified as blood pulsed through his veins.

He stepped out from under the shower, moved to the back of the spacious enclosure and reached again for the soap. Suds slid down his slick skin, through the hair growing low on his abdomen into the thatch cushioning his sex. His hand was warm and soapy when he took his dick in his hand. He leaned his forehead on the forearm he'd braced on the wall and spread his legs.

Water pummeled his back and his buttocks as he began to stroke away the tension he'd had building for days. Eyes screwed up tight, he imagined Erin on her knees, her short sleek auburn hair slicked back, her big silver-bright eyes looking up into his, her mouth forming the perfect O, her lips plump and pink and wrapped around him.

He wanted to get her on her knees. He wanted to see the cherry ripe tips of her breasts pucker and pout. He wanted to know how much of her body she shaved and how her baby bare skin would taste when he sucked her into his mouth.

Sebastian threw back his head and silently roared,

straining beneath the release that grabbed hard between his legs and jerked his lower body forward. He thrust hard, thrust repeatedly, spilling himself into the soap-scented steam when he wanted more than anything to spill himself into the welcome warmth of Erin Thatcher's body.

2

"I'M GOING TO HAVE TO clone myself or forget ever getting the rest of this party planned."

Erin shoved empty mugs and pitchers into a tub beneath Paddington's bar, a full circle in the center of the high-ceilinged room with interior walls of exposed red brick. Booths ran along both the left and the right, and clusters of tables sat scattered across a high-gloss concrete floor that reflected track lighting from overhead beams.

Frustrated, she shoved the heavy glassware a little too hard and ended up splashing beer the length of one pant leg. "Great. Just great." *Count to ten, Erin. Count to ten.* "And, of course, I didn't get to pick up my dry cleaning and don't have a change of clothes in the office."

Cali Tippen, the wine and tobacco bar's number one waitress and Erin's number one friend, dumped her empties into the trash and spun her serving tray onto the bar before offering Erin a commiserating pat on the back along with a clean rag. "Eau de Budweiser, huh? I doubt anyone will notice it over the Parfum Merlot or the smoky essence of *Le Cigare Cubain.*"

"Tell me about it. The smoke in this place? Even with the phenomenal exhaust system I installed during the remodeling, I go home reeking." Erin grimaced.

"And I'm still looking for a daily shampoo I can use daily."

She sighed. She pouted. Neither did her any more good than did the shampoos. She was never going to get over missing Rory. His matter-of-factness. His ribald humor. His huge meaty hands that crushed despair and meted out comfort with the same soothing touch.

A touch Erin longed to feel again. Especially on eat-a-worm days like today when every time she turned around she expected to see him looking over her shoulder, reassuring her that he was happy with the way she was running his place.

His place. Not hers.

She shook off a rush of melancholy. Chin-length strands of hair brushed the skin beneath her ear, a scratchy irritating tickle that renewed her aggravation. "All those specialty hair products and I have nothing to show for the expense but burnt straw."

Cali reached out and tugged on one of Erin's auburn locks. "Your hair is as soft and gorgeous as always. And if you need a change of clothes, I have an extra pair of work pants hanging in the car."

Erin took the rag Cali still held and did what she could to mop up the mess that had soaked into her pant leg from ankle to knee. "I'd take you up on the offer, except for one obvious problem."

Cali paused, frowned, glanced from her ankles to Erin's, from Erin's waist back to her own. "Hmm. Why do I always forget about your long legs?"

"Yes. Erin Thatcher. Redheaded stick figure. I know. I know," Erin groused, tossing the useless rag in the bin when what she really wanted to do was pull out her dry hair by the roots.

Except then she'd be forced to buy a wig and she

couldn't afford to buy herself a beer. Not with this party looming and getting more complicated and expensive every time she turned around.

Enough already!

Her bitchy mood was getting on her own nerves; she couldn't imagine why on earth Cali was still hanging around. Except that best friends did that sort of thing for one another. And right now Erin couldn't have imagined having a better best friend. Or needing one more.

Looking Erin up and down, Cali grinned. "The red hair and the legs, I'll give you. But stick figure? Not a chance. You've got two serious bumps going on upstairs."

Erin smiled and returned the wave of a regular customer, an upscale professional type who'd settled onto one of the bar's swivel-back stools. She moved to draw a draft beer. "I look like one of those long green bugs with bulging headlight eyeballs. At least you have proportions."

"Right? Take two parts short legs, one part J-Lo butt, throw in a couple of perky Britney Spears knockers and there ya have it." Cali handed Erin another frosted mug for one of the Rat Pack wanna-bes needing a refill. "Oh, did I forget to mention the extra fifteen pounds that this recipe *so* does not call for?"

"Puh-lease. You are a walking, talking recipe for s-s-s-sex," Erin teasingly whispered into Cali's ear before delivering the mug to the customer who'd joined his buddies for their daily, post-workday bull session and even now sat cutting the head of a cigar.

Impatiently twirling her tray around on the bar, Cali waited for Erin to get back before growling out a frustrated response. "Being a sex recipe isn't doing me a bit of good seeing as I don't have anyone to cook with."

Her back to the far side of the bar, Erin turned her attention to the girlfriend who'd been her number one rock the past three years and now appeared to need a bit of shoring up herself.

With a surreptitious tilt of her head, she drew Cali's attention to the man behind her sitting alone at the bar. "I'm not sure that sexy blond number back there wouldn't jump at the chance to stir you up."

Blue eyes as bright as the frustrated heart she wore on her sleeve, Cali peered furtively, hopefully beyond Erin's shoulder and sighed. "He is dishy, isn't he?"

And he was.

But Will Cooper was also the study partner Cali had been assigned at the beginning of the fall semester's screenwriting class. That meant an automatic conflict of scholastics and pleasure. As obvious as was Cali's interest in Will, she clearly had reservations about pursuing him outside the boundaries of brainstorming and critique.

Erin looked back at Will—who sat poring over a sheaf of handwritten notes, his head bent, gold oval-framed glasses perched on the end of his nose, the hand holding his yellow number two pencil rubbing back and forth over his spiky, sun-bleached hair—then she turned her consideration to Cali.

"What exactly *is* going on between you and Will? Tell me again why you can't have your yummy man cake and eat him, too?"

Cali rolled her eyes, then gave a little shrug, a little sigh, a little bit of a pout. "Oh, Erin. I like him so much. We have a total blast working together in class. And playing together after class. I don't want to mess that up. Will is a really good friend and good friends don't grow on trees.''

"Good friends can make for good lovers, you know.'' Erin grimaced at the hollow-sounding words. Rather than offering the empathy intended, the sentiment came across as a weak effort at placating her friend's misgivings.

Thank goodness Cali was sharp enough, not to mention knew Erin well enough, to get it anyway. "Well, duh. I wouldn't want a lover that wasn't a friend. But I wouldn't want to lose Will as a friend because we didn't work out together in bed.''

Friends and lovers.

Funny, but Erin hadn't even thought about sharing anything but the joy of sex with her Man To Do. She hadn't thought about introductions and small talk and changing her sheets. She definitely hadn't thought about mornings-after, or face-to-face encounters with the man she wanted only for his body and what he made her body feel.

And that was fine. Absolutely fine. Nothing wrong with a completely physical, emotionally-free affair. She sure didn't have the time or the energy for anything more.

Nose scrunched in thought, she shook her head. "I don't know, Cali. I can't see you and Will having a bit of trouble working things out in bed.''

Cali glanced toward the front door as one of the couples who regularly frequented Paddington's walked through and slipped into their usual booth in the room's darkest corner. She pulled two wineglasses from the rack overhead and picked out a perfect Pinot Noir before sending Erin a pointed glance. "If you're seeing me and Will in bed working at anything then you're nothing but a voyeuristic pervert.''

Erin chuckled. ''The very least of the kinky urges I'm fighting today.''

''And what's that supposed to mean?'' Cali asked, focused on arranging the objects on her serving tray.

Lips pressed together, Erin frowned. It was best friend confession time. As much as she relied on Tess and Samantha for cyber support, a real life girlfriend had the advantage of being able to reach out and smack Erin back to straight thinking.

She took a deep breath and blurted out, ''I'm planning to seduce a man.''

Unfazed, Cali patted her apron pocket and came up with the corkscrew she needed. ''Well, all I have to say is that it's about damn time.''

Leave it to Cali not to mince words, especially when it came to Erin's dating drought of late. Of late? Who was she kidding? More like her dating drought of the last three years. One relationship disaster after another. Men resenting the time she put into Paddington's. Or finding her unapologetically outspoken nature a turnoff.

Which was why her Man To Do fling was not going to be a relationship. It was simply going to be fun. ''True, though this time I'm planning to seduce a man I don't even know.''

''So, you'll find him, you'll get to know him and…bang.'' Cali lifted a brow, lowered her voice. ''So to speak.''

''Well…'' This was where it got more complicated. ''I've decided to skip the get to know him part.''

Cali hoisted the tray onto the flat of one palm and, glaring at Erin, grumbled under her breath. ''Your sense of timing never ceases to amaze me. You always drop your best bombs when my hands are full.''

''I'll fill you in when you get back.'' Grinning, Erin tilted her head toward the dark corner where the couple who'd come in minutes before already sat intimately embraced. ''The Daring Duo is waiting.''

''Well, they'd better keep waiting until I get there.'' Cali gave an exaggerated shudder. ''I *so* do not like walking up on their funny business.''

Erin had a feeling Granddad Rory would've shared Cali's sentiment to the point of giving the couple his famous heave-ho. Then again, if Rory'd still been the one running Houston's Paddington's On Main, the bar would have attracted an entirely different clientele.

Times like this Erin couldn't help but wonder what Rory would think of what she'd done with his dream. Or what he'd think of her. She smacked Cali on her backside, sending her on her way. ''It's not funny business. It's the business of romance.''

Cali skittered two feet away and out of Erin's range. ''Maybe so, but we're in the business of wine and cigars, a little Sade and Dido and even a little U2. Not the business of groping beneath the table.''

Erin delivered a pointed glance in Cali's direction. ''Be thankful Mr. Daring hasn't taken to groping her above the table. And that Ms. Daring hasn't taken to doing a lap dance for him.''

''Trust me.'' Cali shuddered. ''I'll be the first to scream should I walk up on that scenario.''

With Cali gone about her business, Erin glanced the length of the bar. All the customers were set with drinks and in deep enjoyment of rich smoke and good conversation. She glanced out across the dimly lit room, wiping down the bar as she did, and taking pleasure in the richly burnished booth toppers and the lush color scheme of indigo and bloodred wine.

Tonight's crowd was small but the hour was still early. The after-work rush began around six, reaching its peak close to nine. Between nine and eleven, neither Erin nor the servers found but the rare moment to take more than a quick bathroom break. The way she figured, the longer she held it, the more money the cash register was socking away.

Having revamped Rory's beer hall into an upscale establishment better suited to Main Street's revitalized urban scene, she'd done well her first year of operation, not quite turning what could be called a profit, investing what she did make back into the venture, definitely breaking even. Her five-year projection was finally taking on the guise of reality, looking more like an actual business plan every day when she worked on the books.

But if the end-of-month anniversary celebration bombed after her huge financial outlay, she was going to be up a certain creek lacking even the semblance of a paddle to save her sorry hide, not to mention drowning with all those wasted years of Rory's work swirling down the drain behind her.

But she couldn't think about that now. The thinking she did now had to be positive and productive or the resulting stress would put her into a too early grave. The Halloween anniversary party was going to be the talk of the town.

And it damn well better be after all the hair-tearing it had taken to come up with the battle-of-good-and-evil, black-and-white theme. She'd already planned her own mistress of ceremonies costume and only hoped she had the chutzpah to pull it off with half the necessary aplomb.

With Cali making her way back to the bar, Erin sent a quick glance around to find the other servers efficiently covering the tables, affording her a few minutes to slip into the office and drag Cali with her. Taking hold of Cali's hand, Erin didn't give her girlfriend the chance to say no, or what the hell, or anything else.

Once the door shut behind her, Cali pushed a hand back through her short mop of blond Meg Ryan curls and stared at Erin like she'd just taken a leave from her senses as well as from the bar. "You'd better make this fast. I'm afraid to leave The Daring Duo without a chaperone for more than five minutes."

"Here. *This* is what I wanted to show you." Erin picked up the magazine she'd brought with her to work. She flipped to the page she'd dog-eared and handed Cali the article to read.

"Men To Do Before Saying, 'I Do!'" Cali glanced up from the page of five men standing in a line-up, a height chart on the wall behind their heads. They were all over six feet tall. And built. And gorgeous in a male modelicious unreality as opposed to the very real, real-man appeal of Erin's fantasy. "You're kidding me, right?"

"Not at all." Erin's sigh was heavier than she'd intended, especially after swearing off her earlier bad mood. "I'm tired, Cali. Tired of double standards that let men get away with casual flings while focusing on their careers. Tired of working and never having any fun. And, quite frankly, I'm tired of going to bed alone."

Scanning the article, Cali lifted both brows, whether in judgment or in consideration it was hard to tell.

"Okay. I can understand where you're coming from. Having a Man To Do does sound tempting." She caught the corner of her lower lip between her teeth and chewed, then flipped to the second page. "It's just the idea of going for it that would freeze me up. I am too much of a wuss."

"A wuss? You? When did that happen and where was I that I missed it?" Cali's attraction for Will was obviously giving her more trouble than she'd admitted to Erin. And, yeah. Erin could see how it would be tough, deciding whether to answer the call of body or brain.

She gave her best friend an encouraging smile. "You have more guts than anyone I know. That's why I let you hang out with me. I need the moral support and the example. Plus, you make me look really good."

"Does that mean I need to go after Will to show you how it's done?" Cali giggled, her laughter holding a twinge of desperate hysteria to go with her way too-wide eyes.

Aiming to jolt Cali's self-esteem, Erin socked the other woman's shoulder. "It hasn't been that long, moron. I still know the basic tab A into slot B, how-to-ride-a-bicycle mechanics. It's just…"

Cali picked up Erin's trailing sentence. "It's just what?"

Sighing, Erin leaned back against her desk, a hand on either side of her hips. "It's just that damn female inclination to involve emotions. And I don't want to get emotional about this. I don't want to get distracted and obsess over what to wear and whether or not I need to shave and if he's going to call."

Cali simply shrugged. "So, *you* call. And wear what *you* want to wear. And go prickly if you don't feel like shaving. If this is going to be a purely sexual liaison, then don't wig out playing mental games with yourself.''

Erin nodded. Her girlfriend was right. Uncertainty had no place in her personality. Or her plans. Setting her sights on a Man To Do was the perfect example of a positive step toward solving a particular problem. It was not an issue requiring an undue measure of emotional angst.

In fact, it didn't require anything but the involvement of her very ready and needy body. She could do this. She would do this, she thought, and stomped her foot for emphasis. ''You're right. I'm not going to wig out. In fact, this is going to be nothing but fun and games.''

''Good girl.'' With a sigh of finality as she glanced at the article and a shrug as she closed the pages, Cali handed the magazine back to Erin. ''If it goes well for you, who knows? Maybe I'll give it a go.''

''With Will, right?'' Erin so wanted to see the couple together but it was her turn to worry about Cali wigging out over a friend and relationship she couldn't afford to lose.

''We'll see.'' Cali headed for the door, stopping with her hand on the doorknob. ''I think I'll put my study skills to use and observe you from afar, take notes, analyze, form hypotheses and all that.''

Erin teasingly frowned. ''What? You save the close-up examination for The Daring Duo?''

''Ugh.'' Cali screwed up her nose and grimaced. ''Thanks for ruining my sexually upbeat mood with *that* reminder.'' She tugged open the door. ''Your payback will be hell, you know. Along the lines of me never telling you a single detail if I do get busy with Will. So there!''

"Hey! That's not fair." Erin stuck out her tongue in response to Cali doing the same thing before closing the door behind her. Erin chuckled. Sex confessions and childish pranks. The peas and carrots of female friendships. And, speaking of friends...

Before returning to what would no doubt be another busy evening, she took a minute to check her e-mail. She hadn't had a chance yet today to see if either one of her Eve's Apple cronies had responded to her wild Man To Do idea.

It took only a minute for the mail chime to ring and but a few seconds for her to scan through her new e-mails and the Eve's Apple mailing list digest to find a response from Samantha. Erin grinned as she dropped into her chair and tucked one foot up beneath her to read.

From: Samantha Tyler
Sent: Thursday
To: Erin Thatcher; Tess Norton
Subject: Re: Magazine Article on Doing Men

Dear Erin: Men To Do! What an idea! I got this total thrill of excitement when I read your note. Could I use an uncomplicated sex-fest? Um...yeah. With the emphasis on uncomplicated. I am even sick of the *word* "relationship." Compromise, disappointment, crumbling fantasies... I don't sound *bitter,* do I? Well anyway, count me in.

As for The Scary Guy—I don't know. How scary is scary? I mean is he Hannibal Lecter scary or just scary in how he makes you feel? Truth is, I like odd guys. I was always getting crushes on geeks in high school. They had a lot more personality than those gorgeous swaggering butthead jock types. Ha! Swaggering buttheads. Hey! That's the Man To Do I want. The Swaggering Butthead. Whaddya think?

Well, I say go for it—cautiously. Take pepper spray on your dates and if he ever seems *really* scary and not just intriguing-scary, run like hell. As for how to approach him? Erin, this is a guy we're talking about. Just smile! He'll do the rest. And keep us posted on everything. Love, Samantha.

Erin grinned, reading through the e-mail again. Trust Samantha to be so totally Samantha, even when it came to choosing a man for nothing but sex. The Swaggering Butthead, indeed!

Still, he couldn't be any worse than The Scary Guy. The Swaggering Butthead would certainly be easy enough to find. And he'd definitely be predictable.

That was one thing Samantha, Tess and Erin all agreed on. Men did not change, leaving her to wonder what Man To Do type Tess might have chosen—though Erin was quite sure she'd pegged him in her original note.

Closing Samantha's e-mail and scrolling down the rest of her mail, Erin found the note she'd been expecting from Manhattan's very own Green Thumb Goddess.

From:　Tess Norton
Sent:　Thursday
To:　Erin Thatcher; Samantha Tyler
Subject:　Re: Magazine Article on Doing Men

Dear Erin: The Playboy of the Western World? Are you out of your mind? Dash Black is so far out of my league that I'm lucky I get to water his plants. So, okay, I do end up with more than my share of losers, but Brad and I are doing just fine, thank you. He explained about not showing up for our date last night, and hey, that kind of stuff happens, right?

Besides, he's taking me to Robert DeNiro's Tribeca party Christmas Eve. Now all I have to do is find a dress that's priced like Tommy Hilfiger and looks like Versace. Do you think they have Jimmy Choo shoes at the Salvation Army thrift?

As for your Scary Guy? Oh, honey, go for it. Yum. The mind simply reels with the possibilities. The idea is WONDERFUL and you both deserve to let go and have at it. There's a million inappropriate men out there, and they're all just waiting for gorgeous creatures like you to crook your fingers.

Life is short! Eat dessert first! Make it happen. Build yourself some wild memories. Just be careful, okay? Don't go overboard. Think to yourself, "What would Tess do?" Then do the opposite. Love, Tess.

Erin chuckled. Leave it to Tess to shop for Jimmy Choo at the Salvation Army. As if! Erin only wished Tess was here in Houston so the ribbing she deserved could be delivered in person. Sighing, Erin forced herself up from her chair and the e-mail she wanted to answer more than she wanted to return to the bar and all the work she had waiting.

What in the world was wrong with her? She'd lost all her ability to concentrate on Paddington's and too much of her ability to care. At least it seemed that way lately. Maybe a prescription for Prozac was in order.

Or maybe she just needed to get over herself, to suck it up, to remember all the things Rory taught her about living life to the fullest. About not working oneself to death which, for some reason, had become her stock-in-trade of late. "And that wasn't supposed to have happened," she grumbled, shoving both hands back through her hair.

Well, she sure wouldn't let it continue. She was going to get this funk under control and celebrate the bar's success in style. Her bar. Her concept. Erin Thatcher's very own Paddington's On Main. She had to start thinking of this place as hers, instead of looking back expecting to see Rory frowning his displeasure at what she'd done with his place.

She would also have the recreational time of her life with her Man To Do. No complications, no emotional involvement and, echoing the encouraging sporting wear logo, absolutely No Fear. She'd learned more than a few tricks of survival growing up at the feet of Rory Edwin Thatcher and she was not about to let down her granddad even now.

She would *carry on,* prove herself worthy of wearing the Thatcher name and of the gift of Paddington's On Main.

CALI MADE THE ROUNDS of her tables, chatting with customers, refilling orders, fending off the usual spate of come-ons which, thankfully, were few and far between and innocent at that.

She'd definitely been on the receiving end of worse when working at worse places. Meeting Erin and landing this job had been an intervention Cali's life had desperately needed.

Paddington's On Main attracted primarily a two-tiered clientele. First there were the ones Erin—thanks to Will's smart-mouthed observations—referred to as Rat Pack wanna-bes, young and slick and confident male professionals who brought to mind Frank Sinatra and Dean Martin and the rest of the original cast of *Ocean's Eleven.*

Cali wouldn't necessarily have made the connection if Will hadn't been a big fan of old movies. But apparently more than a few, uh, professional females hadn't been as slow on the uptake, she mused, watching hips test the limits of too-tight skirts as the night's manhunt began.

Then there were the couples seeking privacy, low lights and an ambience conducive to illicit assignations. The Daring Duo happened to be the most brazen of the regulars who spent long after-work hours indulging in wine and one another. The others managed to keep their romantic affairs private as romantic affairs should be.

Cali and Erin had fun guessing the nature of the relationships, spinning stories of imagined liaisons, both the origin of the initial attraction and the consequences of the covert tête-à-têtes. Pathetic, really. Two attractive, single, twenty-something women carrying on vicarious trysts rather than experiencing sex in the city.

How those television characters managed to balance careers with all the fun they had Cali would never understand. Between work and school and studying and life's little everyday errands and chores, she barely had time to sleep much less find the energy to be witty and clever and all the qualities required of a femme fatale.

Most of the time it was a struggle to feel *femme.*

Forget *fatale*. But none of that seemed to deter Will Cooper in the least.

He welcomed and respected her input and ideas as they worked on their collaborative screenplay. And he seemed to enjoy her company for her company's sake. After all, it wasn't like by hanging out at Paddington's he was going to get anything cohesive or coherent out of her to add to their idea.

She did good to get the right order to the right customer, forget discussing their project's plot points or determining the value to be switched in a scene.

Finished clearing a vacated table, she turned toward the bar with her loaded tray…only to catch Will's eye. She pulled in a sharp breath, once again amazed at the intensity of the tenderness that tugged at her heart.

The gold frames of his glasses perfectly blended with the sun-kissed color of his hair and the brandied hue of his eyes. He was absolutely beautiful, a description she didn't normally think appropriate for a man. But it fit Will perfectly.

Cali couldn't resist. It was as if she were caught like a fish by a sparkling lure. Dirty dishes and all, she headed that way, reeled in by his sweet look of boyish mischief. His smile nearly brought her to her knees.

And how clichéd was that? One thing she knew well from her creative writing studies was never to settle for the first thing that came to mind, that originality was worth the struggle and the pain.

None of that mattered. Because this was real life, not fiction. And the way Will Cooper looked at her made putting one foot in front of the other a monumental feat of motor skills. She was a complete wreck, her thoughts of Will having strayed into taboo territory after listening earlier to Erin's plans for seducing a man. A man she didn't even yet know.

And Cali knew Will well.

A light shudder settled at the base of her spine as she set the tray on the bar and leaned her upper arm against it, moving as close to Will as propriety allowed, then moving closer—between his stool and the one beside, when his body heat beckoned.

The look on his face, the pensive expression and slightly crooked smile, had her longing to crawl straight up into his lap, wrap her arms around his neck and be done with this hands-off business.

"One of these days you are really going to have to rework your schedule and factor in some time off." Will reached up and tucked an errant curl behind Cali's ear. His hand lingered and then, frowning, he withdrew his touch, a look of uncertain surprise darkening his features—as if he had no idea that his hand had a mind of its own.

Cali did her level best not to scoot even closer and bury her face into the crook where his neck met his shoulder. The temptation of his warmth was hard to ignore. What she did, however, lifting her hand to retrace the path his had taken, was equally revealing. He watched the movement of her fingers, the fluttering motions she made trying to cover her blunder.

Oh, but she wished she was better at hiding her emotions because Will's gaze had snagged on hers and she knew exactly what he was seeing. Her eyes had always been huge and liquid and unable to hide her feelings. And what she was feeling right now was exactly what she didn't want Will to know she felt.

The way her heart tripped through her chest at the thought of his touch, the way her thoughts tripped over one another on the way to her tongue, the way arousal tripped down the length of her spine to settle deep in the core of her belly where she really wished Will would put his hand.

But he was staring and waiting and her hesitation was only making things worse. If only Erin hadn't planted the seed of the idea for seduction. But she had—and now, looking into Will's eyes, standing so close to the stool where he sat, Cali couldn't think of anything else.

She took a step back and strove to appear unaffected. "I get time off. It's just the same nights I have class. *We* have class."

A corner of Will's mouth quirked with a crooked grin. "So how come if we have three nights a week together in class and I hang out here the nights you work that it seems like we don't have any time together?"

"Because we don't have any time together." Cali shrugged even as expectation increased the rhythm of her heart. Was he wanting them to have time together? "We have class time and work time and we try to squeeze studying and brainstorming into snatches that seem about as long as a commercial break."

"Yeah. I know." He fingered another of her stray curls, this time running the back of his hand and his fingers down the side of her throat. "But I was talking about us. Spending time. Together."

"Us? Together? Not working on the screenplay?" Cali had to be sure of what Will was thinking because what *she* was thinking had to be obvious. Her cheeks felt like two stovetop burners turned up high. Was he really suggesting what she'd hoped now for two months he'd suggest?

"Right." He moved his hand back to his beer mug and winked. "Last I knew it was called dating. Or, at least, hanging out."

He'd added the second part when her breath had hitched at the first. His use of the word *dating* had thrown her for a loop. That was all. She hadn't meant to give him pause when she'd paused. She'd only been making sure she was still breathing and that her feet were still on the ground.

"Hanging out sounds great," she said though it sounded like a crummy silver medal compared to the gold of dating Will. Why the hell had she hesitated?

This was it. Now or never. She had two seconds to make her decision because a customer had signaled for a refill on his beer. And then she caught sight of Erin chatting with three white-shirt-and-designer-suited hotties at the bar and that was it.

Man To Do time.

Cali picked up her tray. "Hanging out sounds great. But dating? Now that sounds like heaven."

And then she leaned forward and kissed his bristly cheek, feeling the fire of Will's gaze burning into her back as she walked away.

3

Chapter 4

Raleigh Slater needed to catch up on his shut-eye. The catnaps and midday siestas he'd been surviving on weren't cuttin' it anymore. He needed eight hours. He needed ten. Hell, combine the two and make it an even eighteen. He was running ragged and it was beginning to show.

Not in his work. That wasn't going to happen. He hadn't busted his ass for the biggest part of his life only to turn around and fuck it up by falling asleep on the job. But it was beginning to show in his face.

He dragged a hand down his jaw, needing a shave, afraid, as dog-tired as he was, that he'd slip and slice through his jugular if he put as much as an electric razor to his skin. He stared at his mirrored reflection, realizing the thought actually held a measure of appeal.

One nice clean slash and it would all be over. His career. His life. And the godforsaken wait for the end he'd seen coming since turning down a devil's bargain with the prince of darkness himself. A decision Raleigh was living to regret.

Yep, one good slash and he'd be done with this

*nightmare. And wasn't that exactly what HE was
waiting for Raleigh to do. To take himself out. To
realize the monumental mistake he'd made when
he'd "just said no."*

*That was why HE had sent the woman. Raleigh
should've been faster on the uptake. He'd taken
way too long to figure it out.*

*Every time he turned around she was there,
crossing his line of sight while he sat holed up on
a stakeout, distracting him from the subject at
hand with her long-as-the-Mississippi legs and
amazingly fair skin—considering she lived in a
city where the sun ate and burned flesh with abandon—and her copper-colored hair swinging...*

Copper-colored hair? Fuck. Had he really just written *copper-colored hair?*

Sitting in a booth in a far dark corner of the bar,
Sebastian fingered his pencil until it threatened to snap
under the pressure of angry frustration. He stared at the
yellow legal pad, shook his head and snorted.

The female protagonist in this Ryder Falco novel did
not have copper-colored hair. She was a rare white
blonde befitting her angelic nature. Clichéd, perhaps,
and he might change his mind during revisions. But
one thing was certain.

The red hair he was writing about belonged to Erin
Thatcher and not his fictional heroine.

After another night with less than three hours of
sleep—or had it been daylight when he'd finally
crawled into bed?—he'd decided tonight was the night
he'd make his long overdue visit to Paddington's On
Main. And this time he'd actually walked through
the door.

He'd waited, timing his visit to an hour when he'd known the bar would be busy, wanting to remain undetected as long as he could. The same way he remained undetected when he walked the streets at night—the best way he'd found of getting into Raleigh's skin to move his story forward. So what if Sebastian ended up on the corner across the street from the bar every time, staring through the windows fronting Main Street?

He told himself he needed to observe her in her natural habitat in order to plan his next move. Less of a lion stalking a gazelle and more of a hawk preparing to pluck unsuspecting prey. Though he doubted she was all that oblivious to the sparks biting between them. Not with the way he'd caught her more than once wetting her lips while he watched.

He'd brought pencil and paper to Paddington's and parked his backside in a booth that gave him a full view of the circular bar where she ruled. He liked that about her. That she was a woman in charge of her world.

Confidence was a good thing. Meant she knew what she wanted. Lessened the chances of her being too repressed to answer any questions he asked. Or to reply when he demanded. He wanted to give Erin Thatcher what she wanted. Because making her sweat wasn't going to cut it.

Before he could figure out the source of his obsession, he had to take her to bed.

Erin couldn't breathe. She doubted her lungs would ever start working again and, if they did, she still wouldn't be able to breathe. And, no. It wasn't the cigar smoke asphyxia she'd been anticipating for the past year finally doing her in.

She was totally, freaking paralyzed.

Sweat coated her palms, tickled the small of her back, soaked into the underwire bra she wore beneath her black monogrammed polo. The hair growing low on her nape frizzed; her skin buzzed from the static.

Ten minutes ago she'd been fine. Peachy keen fine. Then she'd looked up and seen him. The Scary Guy, her Man To Do, was sitting in the booth behind The Daring Duo. And, of course, he was facing this way, staring at her, unabashedly watching her every move.

What was he doing here? In a million years she wouldn't buy this as a coincidence. He'd never come in to Paddington's before. She would've remembered. And she couldn't believe he'd randomly picked to-night—less than twenty-four hours after she'd brought herself off to the imagined fantasy of his hands—to visit.

This was too weird. Too totally weird.

She'd sent Cali to take his order—but only after ex-plaining the flush of heat to her face in girlfriend-manspeak. Cali had looked at Erin like she'd lost her mind. *He* was The Scary Guy Erin planned to seduce? He looked like a man who had virgins for dessert, toss-ing them into the volcano for his after-dinner show.

And Erin thought she'd survive sleeping with him? Cali's voice couldn't have screamed, ''Are you crazy?'' any louder than her expression.

And if Cali didn't get back here in the next thirty seconds, Erin was going to cross the room, strangle—then fire—her best friend. What the hell good did it do for Cali to waitress at Paddington's when it took her this long to find out what the man wanted? This was not good for business. Not in the least.

Count to twenty, Erin. Count to twenty.

She could've counted to twenty-two thousand and it wouldn't have been enough of a distraction. She needed something, anything, to ease the sensation of having her every move watched, her figure in her black pants and polo scrutinized, her head of burnt straw studied the way one would inspect a ripe peach before plucking it from a branch overhead.

Ripe peach indeed, she mused, even while admitting her juices were stirred. She couldn't help but wonder if he'd actually visited her dreams. Or if he'd been in her room those minutes before she'd fallen asleep, those minutes when she'd imagined his hands to be the ones slipping into her panties and the folds of her sex.

What other reason would compel him to come here? He couldn't have randomly picked Paddington's to visit tonight, not after the fantasies she'd woven of his mouth and his body. She'd psychically summoned him. That was it. He'd come because she'd mentally called.

And nothing had ever frightened her more.

Yet…this wasn't a Hannibal Lecter sort of scary at all. This wasn't a wet-your-pants sort of scary. At least not the wetting usually associated with fear. No, this was more the stirred juices of a plucked peach, wet-your-panties sort of trepidation. The thought had Erin chuckling at herself. And chuckling at herself was a good thing, right?

Oh, God. Please let laughing be good and not the signal of her descent into demented hysteria.

Where the bloody hell was Cali? How long could it take to take the man's order and make the short walk back to the bar? But Erin didn't dare turn around. Not when she knew she'd be unable to pull off anything resembling disinterest. Because her juices were not the only thing stirred. Her interest was spinning as wildly as the bar's blender on frappé.

Finally, Cali's crepe-soled footsteps sounded around the end of the bar. "Well, well, well." She moved to the cooler and pulled out a bottle of rich amber ale. Rich, imported and expensive amber ale. "I hope you know what you're getting yourself into, girlfriend. You've chosen to do a man with the most excellent taste."

Erin sank into the wide yawn of the floor opening beneath her. Leaning back against the bar, she crossed one arm over her middle and rubbed her forehead with her other hand. "Great. Just great. It's definitely plutonium."

"Say what?"

"Nothing." She waved off Cali's query. "Just trying to decide if I want to back out before it's too late."

"Uh-uh. No backing out." Cali shook her head until her curls heartily bounced. "Not when I've decided to join you in your crazy scheme."

Erin's head came up. "Join me? Now what are *you* talking about?"

"Hold that thought. I've got an order to deliver." Cali inclined her head toward the far side of the bar where the stools were rapidly filling. "And you need to quit slacking off and get back to work."

The rest of the busy weekday evening found Erin and Cali with time to exchange only snippets of conversation, tossing off the verbal shorthand they'd developed during the last year of stepping over and around one another, dodging customers and servers and swinging kitchen doors. The verbal shorthand that helped streamline the bar's operation. The verbal short-hand that was usually enough.

But not tonight. Tonight Erin needed to talk. She counted her lucky stars that it wasn't the weekend or she'd never have managed to find out even the tidbits Cali collected and managed to whisper in passing.

"I'm not sure *what* he's writing," Cali said, exchanging empties for another round of drinks. Erin had noticed his legal pad earlier and sent Cali to snoop. "It looks like an article or a journal. Maybe even a story."

"A story? You're the screenwriter and you can't tell what it is he's writing?" Erin shoved a crate of clean beer mugs beneath the bar. "What am I paying you good money for if you can't even snoop worth a damn?"

"If my salary is your idea of good money, we need to talk," Cali said and scooted out from behind the bar before Erin could get her mouth around a comeback.

She put half her mind back to taking care of the customers clustered around the circular bar. With the hour growing late, the after-work professionals had been joined by the more Bohemian crowd that frequented Paddington's long into the late night hours.

And, why not? Lots of artsy types spent time creating in quiet cafés or corner Starbucks. Even now, Will Cooper sat huddled over his notebook, working to make order from his and Cali's chaotic collaboration, though tonight he seemed more distracted than usual. Interesting that.

So, why shouldn't Erin's Scary Guy find Paddington's to be conducive to his brand of expressive art…if art was indeed what he was writing and not a list of possibilities involving plutonium? Argh, would this night never end?

Getting back to work, she finally talked the Rat Pack wanna-bes into sharing two pitchers so she didn't have to hover near where they sat refilling one mug after another. Usually she didn't mind the fending off of flirty come-ons that were part and parcel of bartending. But tonight she had too much on her mind. And having her Man To Do in the house wasn't helping her state of mind.

For some reason, she found herself less of the confidante or counselor Rory had always been to his regulars—both here in Houston and in Devon's Paddington's. Rory, being the lovable but landlocked seafarer that he was, had spun many a mean yarn while drawing draft beer or pouring shots, yet had known instinctively when to talk and when to listen.

Erin, on the other hand, sold drinks and served drinks and shot the bull or the breeze without inviting any sort of deeper intimacy from her patrons. A part of her wanted to offer more, to be the proprietor of good drink and better conversation Rory had been.

She wanted her granddad to be proud of what she'd accomplished. Instead, she often felt he wouldn't approve, that she'd *carried on* but at the expense of his vision. And that left her conflicted and more than a little bit blue.

Tonight she had less than her usual cadre of wits, so making chitchat offered zero appeal. Still, welcoming any and all distractions, she allowed herself to be drawn into several of the conversations. Any excuse to stay busy, focused on work, and avoid freaking out over The Scary Guy, wondering why he'd come here, what he wanted from her and why he hadn't yet come to get it.

More carefully this time, she cleared several empty

mugs and snifters from the bar and was seriously wiping the finish from the surface when Cali next wedged her way between the cooler and Erin's backside.

"Definitely a story of some sort," Cali said, grabbing a second bottle of ale. "Dialogue markings and short paragraphs. Could be an eyewitness account of The Daring Duo. Though, if it is, I hope they never find out. They don't need any further encouragement, thinking we're actually enjoying their show or anything."

"Good grief. What are they up to now?" Erin's mental gears switched from the first subject to the second but Cali was gone again before she could answer. So, back to The Scary Guy Erin's mind went.

And what if Cali was wrong? What if it wasn't a story at all? What if he was a restaurant critic? Not that she served food worth a critic's time and effort. Her simple fare was just that. Simple. Desserts and appetizers perfectly suited as complements for a bottle of wine. No, what she was selling was the ambience, exactly how she'd learned to do from Rory, though definitely not the ambience he'd sold.

An ambience The Daring Duo was taking *way* too much advantage of, Erin noticed. The two couldn't get their mouths far enough apart to respond to Cali's query about a second bottle of their favorite Pinot Noir. Erin didn't even want to think about what they were doing with their hands.

At the thought of hands, she made the mistake of glancing toward the next table—and found her Scary Guy's focus not on the legal pad in front of him, but on her face, his gaze a bold and steady test of her ability to hold up under a scrutiny that was not the least bit chaste but oh, so, incredibly heady. Her fingers curled into the rag she held and squeezed.

She'd thought him intimidating when they'd passed one another near their building's bank of elevators. She'd thought him threatening when watching in her rearview mirror as his big black muscle car rolled behind her compact Camry into the parking garage.

But the truth of the matter was that on none of those occasions had she felt a fraction, a hint, a trace of the tremors now scuttling down her spine. Tremors that worked their way into the pit of her belly, spreading down between her legs in damp anticipation as she silently accepted his unspoken invitation. Oh, but she was going to die with the waiting.

His eyes were bright, a mad sort of glittering green seeing so many things she worked to hide. Things she hadn't told Cali. Things she would never have told Rory. Things she hated telling herself. But things he so easily divined, capturing and holding her with nothing more than a look.

But, oh, that look. It wasn't hot; it was compelling. It wasn't smoldering or steamy; it was devouring, possessive. Intense in a way that urged her pride to check her hair for flyaway strands, her face for a blemish or a scar. Her psyche for fears she wanted him to explore. She hated, hated, hated the vulnerability. And still she wanted to take off her clothes and give him what access he chose to take.

Suddenly, watching him there as he watched her, her chest felt too small to contain the swell of her fast-beating heart. Her skin burned, as if the touch of his gaze was a physical contact and not the mere suggestion of one. The pits of her arms, the backs of her knees, the valley between her breasts. Perspiration blistered and itched. The creases between hips and thighs grew equally damp. She was literally on fire.

How she survived the rest of the evening she had no idea. But she did, making the requisite bartender chit-chat, removing and refilling glasses and mugs, all the while watching the clock over the front door, the huge clock fashioned from the top of the original Paddington's bar, tick its way toward 2:00 a.m.

The Scary Guy she was determined to know better was one of the last patrons to leave the bar for the night.

Will, as usual, hung around waiting for Cali. And Cali always helped Erin close. The three of them had laughed and cut up as usual while wrapping things up and, between Erin's last two trips to the kitchen, *he* had disappeared.

Finally, she'd been able to breathe, lock up the bar for the night and take herself home.

She had no idea if he'd returned to their shared building but a few blocks down Main, or if he had taken himself off to a club that catered to creatures of the night. And that's exactly what he reminded her of, dressed the way he always dressed in dark colors from head-to-toe, and lean in a way that reminded her of an animal on the hunt and always hungry.

He haunted her, and that's why she'd decided to take this bat by the wings and introduce herself the very next time their paths crossed. She'd kick herself forever if she didn't. And, besides. Saying hello was probably the least etiquette required before she and the man embarked on her premeditated fling.

She pulled her Camry into the building's garage and drove up one ramp after another until she reached the fourth level. Paddington's was within walking distance from the loft and the neighborhood was no worse here than in dozens of other parts of the sprawling metropolis.

But the middle of the night was still the middle of the night, whether downtown or in the burbs. And, quite frankly, Erin valued her safety too much to tempt fate, or any lurking criminal element.

She grabbed up her backpack by one strap, slinging it over her shoulder while hitting the auto lock on the Camry's key chain. The locks clicked and she stuffed her keys down into her front pocket. And then she heard it. In the next second. Between her first step toward the garage elevator and the second. She heard the sound she'd been waiting for, the sound she'd been hoping to hear.

A low rumbling purr, a growl that grew louder as the panther-sleek car approached. Dark-as-night black paint. Tinted windows. Shiny wheels and two cylindrical exhaust pipes to match. She remained still, standing where she'd stopped in her tracks seconds before, her hand wrapped in a death grip around the strap of her backpack draped over her shoulder.

The car crept by, a slow-rolling machine built for power, for pursuit, an intimidating shadow stalking every move she made. Foreboding settled into Erin's belly like a heavy weight, grounding her feet to the hard concrete floor. Her gaze remained on the driver's window from which only her reflection stared back.

But she didn't need to see his face to feel the effects of the look she knew he'd directed her way. The electricity remained, the sizzling, popping burn of her overheated imagination and her body that had yet to shake off last night's erotic dreams.

With practiced ease, the car slipped into the parking

space at the end of the row. Erin hesitated for several seconds, knowing this was it. The chance she'd been waiting for. The chance she had to take. As soon as he killed the engine and the rumble died and the echo of all that horsepower stopped ringing in her ears, she headed for the elevator.

Once inside, she waited. Her back to the side wall of the elevator car, she waited. Holding down the door-open button, her heart hammering hard on her ribs, she waited. Listening for the approaching footsteps, heavy in the black boots he wore.

Or so she'd assumed they must be.

But she'd assumed wrong because he silently rounded the corner and moved into the elevator's tiny square of remaining space before she had a chance to whip her hand away from the panel. He caught her waiting there. And the only thing she could do in response was smile.

So she smiled, and then she looked down because she'd lost her voice. At least she'd lost the ability to say anything intelligent or coherent. And she didn't think telling him to strip to his skivvies was any way to break the ice—even if she wanted more than her next breath to see him naked.

She didn't know enough about men's clothing to guess his size but his boots were absolutely huge. Deep indigo jeans, nearer black than blue, bunched over the boots around his ankles. And, oh, but his legs were long.

Erin's gaze made a slow climb, lingering for what was probably too long for prudence yet not long enough for prurience on his sweetly thick thighs and the equally compelling bulge behind the crotch of his button-down jeans. If only he'd turn around and complete the picture by giving her a nice close-up view of his backside.

But there was no time.

In seconds they'd reach the ground floor. She had to make her move and make it now. A deep breath did nothing to calm her nerves, only served in fact to rattle her further. She tried again, producing a smile she hoped showed at least a small degree of the sultry sensations giving birth to tremors that ran down her spine to the soles of both feet.

But then the bell dinged and the door opened and she had no choice but to exit and hope he followed. He did. He followed even when she bypassed the main building's elevator and headed for the mailroom in the basement. She felt him behind her like the ethereal kiss of a shadow, a warmth with no substance but that which her wanton imagination bestowed.

A rich hunger stirred to life in her belly, accompanied by the twisting and turning of nerves knotting into a near painful anticipation. The short, dimly lit hallway echoed with their alternating footsteps, hers almost louder than his. The air inside sizzled with blue white waves of electrical pulses. The scent of imminent danger burned with a pungent intensity and caused her nostrils to wildly flare.

Then she caught a second scent. The barest trace of an exotic cologne, an expensive blend of green woods and spice. His scent. And the first time she'd been so aware of his individual, unique, arousing allure. She shuddered then, holding the feeling close as desire blossomed and as she stepped into the mailroom and headed for her box.

He made his way straight to his and Erin could barely concentrate on separating junk mail from bills as desperation grew. Never again would she have a more perfect chance than this one. The hour was late and they were both alone and unattached. Two healthy sexual beings lacking a single reason to say no.

Unless he didn't want her. Didn't find her desirable. Unless she'd imagined the earlier sparks spitting and popping in Paddington's air.

She took a deep determined breath and slammed her mailbox door resoundingly. Then she turned, pausing at the trash bin to toss out flyers and sales papers and the postcard reminder from her gynecologist. The rest of the mail she tucked into her backpack, zipping it closed just as the second mailbox door slammed shut. Three footsteps brought him to the trash bin where he tossed the same junk mail she'd discarded.

The rhythm of her heartbeat was pure rock 'n' roll as she lifted her chin and raised her gaze to meet his.

"Hi," she said, her voice amazingly steady when hunger had her weak at the knees. "I'm Erin. Erin Thatcher. I decided it was time I introduced myself considering we're about as close as neighbors can be, you living above me and all."

His eyes were the clear sort of green of old Coke bottles, a beautiful contrast of light against lashes and brows an indisputably rich gothic black. His upper lip was narrow, his bottom lip full, giving his smile an innately sexy and boyish appeal. Nothing else about him, however, could be mistaken as belonging to anyone but a man.

His gaze that still boldly met and held hers never wavered. Neither did he flirt, or tease, or pretend to sidestep what they both so obviously wanted. Amazing how the want was so obvious. Like sex between them wasn't even a question but was a foregone conclusion, a decision made long before this moment, a reality that neither had any say in defining.

Then, in a voice that sounded as if he rarely had reason to speak, in a voice that reminded her of his car's powerful engine idling at a low RPM, in a timbre that held enough resonance of simmering emotion to reassure her she wasn't out of her mind, he told her his name was, "Sebastian Gallo."

Right before he lowered his head.

It wasn't his kiss she found unexpected. She'd been ready for this since before her fantasies had stripped the both of them bare. What she hadn't anticipated was the hunger he was able to restrain. She felt the tension in the barest brush of his lips to hers, in the distance he kept between them even while standing so close.

Her body came alive and the hands that had been holding the strap of her backpack moved to hold on to him. He was tall and he was solid, his biceps beneath her palms as unyielding as stone. She had to lift her chin, lean back her head, stand on the balls of her feet to reach him. And she was not a short woman.

But the way he settled his hands at her hips—his hands, heavy with warmth and confident possession, his hands that were long-fingered and broad-palmed and were the hands of her fantasy—made her feel tiny and feminine and desired. And then, as if the test was complete and time had come to explore the extent of her willing nature, his kiss deepened, grew hard and hungry and his hands pulled her body flush to his.

She knew she was going to die. Her skin burned with a fever too hot for a body to bear. Her heart thumped with an unimaginably hard rhythm and any moment she expected her ribs to crack. The pressure in her chest was that intense. But neither that pressure nor that burn had anything on the ones clawing and growling deep in her sex.

The moisture she knew to be musky and hot soaked into the crotch of her panties. She wanted more than anything to spread her legs wide open. She wanted Sebastian Gallo to slip his hand between her thighs, to finger flesh damp and swollen both inside and out.

She wanted to feel his mouth, his mouth making wild magic with hers, the very same mouth she wanted more than anything to tease and release the explosive nerves drawn taut.

She wanted all of that. She wanted more. And so far they'd shared no more than a kiss. She wondered how she would ever survive the bump and grind of sex. He took a step into her body, pushing her into the waist-high sorting table that ran the length of the mailroom wall. The sharp edge cut into the center of her back. Cut harder when he pressed harder, pushing his full length against her, grinding a most impressive erection into the soft give of her belly.

Tongues tangled, warm breath mingled. Noses bumped, teeth clashed. Erin slipped her arms beneath his and moved her hands to his back then down to his backside, squeezing and urging him forward, closer. She wanted him closer. But clothing and location stood in her way.

And frustration mounted because there was nothing she could do but stand still beneath his touch and...oh, oh, yes, right there, she silently begged, easing her thighs apart when he wedged his knee between. She couldn't breathe. She couldn't breathe. His mouth was stealing too much of her air. The world tumbled away from beneath her, but his thigh between hers kept her from falling.

How could she have known he would taste like this? Like forbidden fruit, sweet and smooth, addictive. Warm sugar melting like heaven on her tongue. The taste of heat and velvet honey.

Yet this kiss, this press of lips, this open-mouthed exploration of tongues and teeth, nibbling and nipping, was an appetizer leaving her hunger to be sated. Leaving desire to be satisfied. Leaving the ache between her legs to be soothed.

He pulled away, panting, struggling. Choppy breaths, both ragged and raw, blew over the skin of her neck. She shuddered, pulled her arms back between their two bodies and curled her fingers into the material of his shirt. She buried her face against the backs of her hands. She didn't know whether to hold on to him forever or to let him go.

The one thing she did know, the one thing that was not in question, was that she wanted more. And so she lifted her head and she looked into his eyes and she smiled, encouraging him to respond similarly.

But his face remained solemn, even when he lifted a hand and brushed wild strands of hair away from her face. Then he leaned forward slowly, brushed his lips tenderly to the corner of one eye and rested his forehead on hers. "Nice to meet you, Erin Thatcher."

Oh, the sound of her name in his mouth. "The pleasure is all mine," she managed to get out before her voice or her legs collapsed completely.

And then he chuckled, lifting Erin's spirits and saying, "That's good to hear. I was hoping I wasn't the only one getting off on this."

"No, this is definitely a mutual mailroom mauling," she said and pulled in a deep shuddering breath.

And then he hooked an arm around her neck and made sure he had her attention before he asked, "So what do you say we take this party upstairs?"

4
_____

ERIN BRACED HERSELF against one wall of the main hotel elevator she used to access her loft. Sebastian leaned against the opposite, legs crossed at the ankle, hands braced behind him, head angled back and chin lifted. His gaze never wavered or left her face.

And that caused her to smile. A nervous smile, she admitted, yes. But the upward pull of her lips was still a smile—one of pure excitement.

She tried not to shuffle her weight from one foot to the other, to switch her backpack from left shoulder to right, to hold in her stomach, hold up her head, straighten her shoulders and her flyaway hair. It was so damn hard to stand still beneath a scrutiny that intense.

How could eyes colored so soft a green, burn with that crystal-sharp edge?

The building elevator's ambience added to the atmosphere of rich expectation. The dark paneled walls, the thick red and gold carpeting, the reflective ceiling of light. Each seemed yet another lush assault on her senses. There was barely enough air for the two of them to breathe.

When they'd stepped inside, not having said a word on the way to the elevators from the mailroom, Erin had let Sebastian take the initiative. Let him take, what a laugh. He'd done exactly as he'd damn well pleased, stepping into the small space behind her and automatically pressing the button to his floor.

She would've loved to sink beneath his weight into her own plush bed, to pull her quilt over their bodies and learn his touch in the private sanctuary of her bedroom. She could imagine the scent of candles burning, the smell of his exotically spiced skin, of his musky warm arousal, the low burning light reflected in his eyes.

Yet, even more than any of those dark desires, she was dying to see his loft, to learn what she could about him from his possessions, his surroundings, the way he lived. She'd wondered for months now about the way he lived. But not half as much as she'd wondered about the way he made love.

The elevator began its slow upward climb and Sebastian took a step forward, and then another. One more brought him within inches of where she stood and she curled her fingers into her fists. Both of his hands moved to the wall above her shoulders, a trap from which she had no desire to escape.

What she had, instead, was a longing for his kiss.

She lifted her chin, parted her lips and his head came down—but only to rub his cheek to hers, bristly skin chafing soft, even as he moved one hand from the wall to her shoulder and squeezed.

The elevator rose higher. Sebastian's hand drifted down, lower, lower still, pressing the flesh above her collarbone before moving to cup her breast. She pulled in a sharp hitch of a breath.

He measured the weight and the fullness, skated the flat of his palm over her pebbled nipple, teasing her with a touch that held incredible promise. She shuddered where she stood, wanting to return the favor, to learn the feel of his body beneath his clothes.

But she stood unmoving. Waiting. Her heart beating. Waiting. His warm breath against her neck sent a sweep of sensation to play over her skin. Shivers raised gooseflesh along her arms, prickling at her nape and her nipples tightened further.

He grinned. She felt the movement of his lips even as he moved forefinger and thumb to lightly pinch and tug. She couldn't help it. Desire rolled up from her belly and she groaned, the sound a murmured hum against his jawline where her mouth rested.

He nuzzled his cheek to her lips as his hand slid lower, measuring her waist. Lower still, to the flat of her belly. And even lower, where his finger found the seam of her pants that ran between her legs and pressed upward, directly against her clit.

She panted and whimpered and barely stopped herself from begging him to get down on his knees. What he did instead caused a missed beat to the rhythm of her heart, even while her blood ran hot and heavy in her veins. He released the button at her waistline, pulled her zipper down, all the while holding her upper body against the wall with the weight of his.

His hand moved into her pants, his skin smooth, his aim sure, as his fingers breached the elastic band of her bikini panties, slipped down to find the plump lips of her sex and her clitoris tight and hard and aching. She nipped at his neck and her fingers gouged into the muscles of his shoulders. She shuffled her feet, opened her legs, allowed him access, lifting upward and…

Oh, yes. Right there. He'd found the one spot, ooh, yes, there. She hitched her hip to the side. Sebastian's finger, one at first, then two, slipped deep, deeper, filling her, withdrawing almost on her next breath, entering again to tease the soft pillow where sensation centered.

He repeated each motion, fingering her like the pleasure was his more than it had ever been hers to enjoy. That thought, that realization that he loved what he was doing hit her hard, a strike on her too-vulnerable female emotions when she'd sworn to keep this encounter emotion free.

Too late, her mind screamed even as her body went over the edge. She shuddered, shook, trembled, shivered, clutching whatever part of him she could find to hold on to. Unbelievable. Oh, oh, she couldn't…oh, his hand, his fingers, big and thick, and she never wanted him to stop. *Don't stop, don't ever stop.* And the spasms continued, rocking her through an orgasm that threatened to buckle her knees and take her to the floor.

Oh…my, she thought, slowly coming back down from a high chemicals could never produce, regaining her physical balance but certain the rest of her equilibrium would never again be so steady. He'd just fingered her to orgasm and they were standing in a bloody elevator, the doors wide open—though when that had happened she hadn't a clue.

Slowly, Sebastian withdrew his hand, his touch still intimately insistent as he pulled away from her sex, lingering along her plump lips, spreading juices to her clitoris as he circled the tiny pearl, wanting her to know what she'd done, what he'd done, that they were nowhere close to being finished.

If anything about him truly scared her—Erin mused, as she adjusted clothing and brushed hair back from her face—it was the way he'd so thoroughly breached any defenses she'd had that she couldn't remember if they'd been there to begin with.

When had another man, any of the men she'd thought herself in love with, ever drawn this physical reaction from her?

She'd certainly had her fair share of sex and probably more than her fair share of orgasms, she thought, accepting Sebastian's hand at the small of her back as he stepped from the elevator and guided her down the hallway.

She'd never been reticent to demand she get hers. And, yes. The drought had been ongoing for quite a long time, but that didn't exactly explain what had just happened, the way she'd let go.

Or why this man—this man with whom she wanted nothing but a physical relationship—had been the one to so boldly blow away any inhibitions she might've had and sweep her up into a wild affair.

She was still working to collect her thoughts and her composure when they reached his front door. He pulled a remote entry key from his pocket, pressed the electronic combination and the lock clicked in response.

Before he pushed the door open, however, he moved his hand from the small of her back, lifted his arm and hooked his elbow around her neck.

He forced her head up, and the first shot of alarm skittered along her hairline, tiny pringles of uncertainty warning her to be on her guard. It wasn't too late to back out. She'd run if she had to. She'd scream. She'd—

"Erin." He caught hold of her gaze, made certain he had her full attention before he said, "We can stop this. It's not too late to stop this."

Wow. That certainly wasn't what she'd expected.

She almost didn't know what to say in response, though she did feel an easing of her nerves. "I'm not too sure about that, Sebastian. Neither the mailroom nor the elevator will ever be the same."

He shook his head, his eyes sparkling beneath those dark-as-night lashes. "I'm not talking about the building. I'm talking about you. I don't want you to regret…"

"What we've done?" She wasn't sure why he'd let the thought trail, but she needed him to know she was fine. And that she was fine with what they were doing. "I don't regret a thing we've done."

He shook his head again and this time his hand moved to caress her neck, his finger traveling down her jugular to her neck and into the hollow of her throat. "I'm not talking about what we've done, but what we're going to do."

The way he said it… The way he touched her… Erin couldn't breathe. She couldn't swallow. The look in his eyes wasn't gentle. Neither was it kind, but demanding and predatory, fantastically hungry, wildly hot.

What would happen, she wondered, if he were to lose control? If she told him she'd been waiting for weeks for what they were going to do? If she admitted she'd wondered what had taken him so long?

But since she couldn't find but the barest hint of a voice, she only managed to say, "Let's go inside."

SEX OR NO SEX, bringing Erin Thatcher into his home was not the way to work the woman out of his system. He should've known that. After their kiss in the mailroom—the kiss a mistake he wouldn't make again—he should've had the common sense to see her to her own front door and say good-night.

But he hadn't.

Instead, after her explosive reaction to his touch in the elevator, he'd brought her straight to his front door. A door no one ever entered. And now he stood back and watched as she stepped over his well-guarded threshold and into Ryder Falco's private domain.

Sebastian wondered how long he would manage to keep his identity a secret. Or how long it would take him to lose the rest of his mind. Insanity was his only defense for allowing her to walk through his door and into his life.

Insanity, and his dick that felt as if it would snap in half if he took another step. Then there were his balls that, by now, had to be an unholy shade of blue.

He leaned back against the closed front door and watched as she studied his living space. He didn't have a lot for her to see. A long, black leather sofa. A sound-system-intensive entertainment center. That was about it.

The rest of the main room's walls were lined with shelves that held hundreds, maybe thousands, of hard-back volumes. He'd never been a paperback kind of guy. Especially not when he could afford to buy what he wanted whether he needed it or not.

Bestsellers, classics, research books, his entire Ryder Falco backlist. The rolling library ladder currently sat parked beneath a section devoted to paranormal occurrences. Now he wondered if he might've done better studying up on how, when so many before her had tried and failed, one woman had managed to work her way into the core of his psyche. He really was a sick bastard, letting it happen.

She moved into the room slowly, hesitantly, obviously unsure what she'd encounter. After all, she didn't know a thing about him, other than the fact that he knew his way around the female body. He assumed that was the reason she was here. For the sex. He wasn't going to fool himself into thinking she was here for him.

No one had ever been here for him.

"You don't have a television."

Strange that that would be her first observation. "Nope. Not a set in the place."

"I don't have one either. Well, there is one in Paddington's office. I read." She gestured around the room at his never-ending bookshelves. "Obviously not as much as you do," she added with a laugh. "I belong to a reading group online. I love seeing how a handful of readers can hold so many opposing views on a book."

She was nervous. Funny. She hadn't been the least bit jumpy in either the mailroom or the elevator. But now that they were here, now that he'd let her put what space she needed between them, she was nervous.

"Yeah. I like books." It was about all he could think of to say.

The corner of her mouth quirked upward. "I noticed."

She slowly walked toward the closest shelves, scanning the titles, mouthing the words she read, frowning, smiling, enjoying her discoveries which drew the ball in his gut even tighter. Appreciating her silent enthusiasm came a little too close to getting into her mind. And it wasn't her mind into which he wanted to find himself buried an hour from now.

When she reached for a book to pull from the shelf, he pushed away from the door and made his way to her side. To her back, actually, hovering in a way he figured she'd respond to as threatening. His portrait on the back of his book jackets was shadowed and dim, but he didn't want to take a chance on her pulling the copy of *The Demon Takes a Lover* from its slot on the next shelf above.

For a moment she hesitated. Then she slid the book she'd removed back into its place. After that, she waited, her eyes drifting closed as she blew out a long breath that Sebastian took to mean she was ready. He lifted the strap of her backpack from her shoulder and set the heavy canvas tote on the floor. Then he settled his hands on her shoulders, replacing the weight of her backpack with the weight of his touch.

She smiled, a gentle expression he felt in places he wasn't supposed to feel a thing. And her eyes were still closed when she raised her hands to cover his there where they rested. "Are you going to show me the rest of your place?" she asked, turning in his arms as she did.

He took a step away. Instinct told him she'd been but a moment from rising up for his kiss. The kiss in the mailroom had been calculated and of purpose. To gauge her intent and reaction, her willingness of body, her state of mind.

But he'd succeeded on one or two of the levels because he'd been the one caught off guard. So, no more kisses for now. Not until he had a better handle on where she was coming from. "There's not much left to see. Nothing more than the kitchen, the bedroom and the bath. And the cat," he added, as Redrum skulked passed.

Erin's gaze followed the black cat until the arrogant fur ball disappeared into the kitchen. The she looked his direction again, a tiny smile tilting at the corner of her mouth. "I know this is going to sound strange, but I would kill for a hot shower before we, uh, do what you've promised we're going to do." She gave a small shrug. "It's the bar. The smoke. And, yes. I sweat while I'm working."

He'd tasted her sweat there on her neck and caught the scent of smoke in hair that smelled of rich herbs. Both had been noticeable, but neither overpowering, appealing to his enjoyment of Erin as a woman.

But the thought of seeing her naked under his shower appealed even more. She could never know how much.

"That's not a problem," he said, gesturing toward the back of the loft. "And not even any killing involved."

"Well, my bark is really much worse than my bite," she said and fell into step beside him.

They avoided his dump of a kitchen and she didn't say a word as she took in the state of his bedroom, the way he'd tossed his comforter up over his bottom sheet and called it making his bed. The pile of worn clothing he hadn't yet taken to the laundry. The notebooks and papers and research texts scattered across his workstation that took up more room than the bed.

A quick glance reassured him nothing she could see would reveal his identity. No, she remained silent, pensive, at least until she got her first look at his bathroom.

Then her jaw totally dropped.

It took her at least a full minute of looking around to find her voice, or to decide what it was she wanted to say. Sebastian understood her awe. He'd felt much the same speechless amazement when he'd finally seen the finished design of his dream the first time.

She covered her mouth with both hands, shaking her head as she looked around the room of chrome and etched glass and black-flecked gray marble. The sleek, onyx floor had her toeing off her work shoes to indulge in the coolly sleek surface.

"And I thought my bathroom decadent." She shook her head. "This is amazing. No, hedonistic. I may never want to leave." She ran the tip of one finger over the deep curve of a chrome faucet. "I have a thing about bathrooms, you know."

No. He didn't know. He only knew that he did.

She moved into the shower space and he shut the door behind him. The click of the latch echoed as always in the cavernous room, a sound he associated with solitude and safety. Never before had he chosen to share the ritual of his shower. And he had to push away the sharp clutch of awareness of that fact demanding explanation, why this woman, why here and now.

An easy answer. Sex.

Nothing less than sex. Certainly nothing more than exploring this rabid obsession.

He moved away from the door, through the dressing room and past the vanity counters and into the shower's main space. A sunken hot tub sat unused in one corner. For Sebastian, this room was all about pulsing jets of hot spray beating down from all sides.

And now it was about Erin Thatcher, to see how far he could take her, to see how far she would go. And, once shed of clothes and inhibitions, to see if they could fuck themselves free of the connection they shared—a hot, biting arc of shocking awareness getting in the way of his life.

ERIN TOOK A DEEP BREATH and, hands clenched, turned to face him. She watched while he pulled off boots and socks, tossing the lot halfway across the room. She watched while he reached for the hem of his navy blue Henley pullover and tugged it off. She watched while he freed the button fly of his jeans and skinned the denim down his legs.

Finally, he stood wearing boxer briefs, black, with a pouch that cupped the soft sac of his balls yet barely held the swollen length of his cock.

She wondered how hard a human heart could actually beat in response to arousal. How fast blood could rush to the parts of her body responding to the gorgeous vision of this near naked man standing not four feet away.

His arms were long, roped with tendons and muscles; the round of his shoulders defined their breadth. His legs were those of a runner, his calves firmly developed, his thighs strong, his feet sporting the barest tufts of dark hair. The same dark hair that grew low in soft swirls on his abdomen.

His stomach and chest were smooth, lightly sculpted and a temptation to touch. She curled her hands into fists and struggled to evenly breathe. And then he moved toward her. That body she'd only seen in head-to-toe dark clothing was now so real and so bare and so incredibly, beautifully hers to explore.

His hands went to the front of her shirt and he pulled the hem from where it had been tucked back into her pants. She let him strip it off, wishing she'd worn lacier underwear, knowing the plain black stretch cups of her bra molded nicely to her curves but weren't particularly sexy. She decided Sebastian didn't care, as he took the weight of her breasts in his hands and tugged the peaks to attention.

She reached for the clasp at her back, wanting to

feel his skin and his mouth, his lips, his teeth, his tongue, but he shook his head to stop her. She let him, hating that she had to wait, loving that she had to wait.

He reached for the button at her waistband, his fingers warm against the skin of her torso, his breath even hotter when he leaned down to blow a stream of air across her taut nipples. The distraction failed to pull her attention from his hands moving into her pants.

When her zipper went down and the heat of his skin warmed her bared belly, shivers set in. She held on to his shoulder as he leaned toward her to pull off her pants, one hand working its way over her backside, the other teasing her front while sliding down the boring black gabardine.

She wasn't sure how she was going to survive sex with this man when having him take off her clothes nearly brought her to her knees. And this bathroom. It was as if showering in and of itself was an afterthought. The room was built for sex. She wondered how many women had been here before her. She wondered if she really wanted to know.

And, now that she stood here in her plain black bra and black athletic panties cut high on the thigh, she wondered why she was wasting time wondering anything at all.

Sebastian straightened. Erin dropped her hand from his shoulder and caught a glimpse of their reflection in the mirror behind. A smile touched her mouth and Sebastian turned to follow the direction of her gaze.

The lift of his lips was less appreciative than suggestive and gave him the hungry look belonging to a bird of prey. She couldn't help herself. She stepped back into his body. "What do you think? Perfect as models for Calvin Klein?"

He shook his head, moved his hands to rest on her shoulders. "I don't think we're looking at the same thing."

She was looking at the contrast of black on white, cotton on flesh, the darker skin of his hands on her fair shoulders. Good and bad in a moment worthy of Kodak. Or, better yet, Zalman King's *Red Shoe Diaries*. This was the moment before the thrill.

She shuddered to think of being stared at, even while she couldn't tear her gaze away. "Tell me what you see. Then I'll tell you mine."

"You'll tell me your what? Your fantasies, maybe?" A dark brow arched. "The ones you have of you and me?"

Arrogant beast. "You think you star in my fantasies?"

"Isn't that why you're here?"

She remembered why she was here and wit escaped her. All she could think of was that he had to know that she dreamed of him, that she'd taken him to bed dozens of times in her mind.

"Am I here for the fantasy?" She met his reflected gaze squarely. "This certainly isn't reality, is it?"

"Depends on how real you want it to be."

They were talking in circles. But, fantasy or reality, she needed ground rules—though better late than never seemed a backward way to work. "Honestly? I want this to be mind-blowing. But I want to know I can walk out of here whenever I'm ready to go. Even if I want to go now."

Sebastian's eyes glittered. His hands slipped over her shoulders and down her arms to her wrists. Then he stepped back and away, leaving her body bereft of his warmth. The upward tilt of his mouth wasn't humorous or cynical, but seemed to signal his acceptance of the reality she'd defined.

Still, she couldn't help but look when he moved his hands to the waistband of his briefs. She caught the barest glimpse of the slitted tip of his erection before he shucked the shorts down his legs and opened her eyes to the amazing dimensions a man's body could take.

Her sex opened and swelled and she had to stop herself from reaching back and copping the feel she so wanted to take. She didn't have time to do more than ogle, however, because he stepped around her, brushing her hip with the edge of his, and pulled the top from a black lacquer box on the vanity.

"I'm going to shower," he said to her reflection in the mirror. "You're welcome to join me."

And that was it. He stepped up into the shower enclosure that wasn't enclosed at all. She counted as, one, two, three, the shower heads blasted on and, in seconds, steam began to rise.

Hot. That's all she could think of. Hot water, hot skin, hot sex. A man hotter than any she'd ever known. This chance was one she'd never have again and was exactly the one she'd been wanting. No ties. No expectations. No regrets.

One deep breath later, she walked to the vanity, peered into the box and thought wicked thoughts as she reached for a handful of condoms.

Who was the scary one now, she mused, and turned toward the shower.

SEBASTIAN STOOD BENEATH the center showerhead, his forehead pressed against the arm he'd braced on the wall. The water beat down on his back as he waited.

He knew she'd come. He'd always known she'd come. They'd played this game now for months and by morning would have gotten what they wanted.

He just had to make sure his twisted mind didn't attempt to take things any further, to imagine an involvement that wasn't there. This wasn't a fictional creation. He didn't need to supply deep motives for either of their choices.

He needed to purge his mind of this distraction, finish up his current Slater contract, then do what he could with the germ of a story idea his muse had planted so he could get the insistent bitch off his back. As motivation, he figured it worked.

And Erin, well, he didn't know what brought her here. Her reasons were her own and unimportant to his plans. But, when he felt her at his back, he forgot about every reason but the one that mattered, the one throbbing like a wild thing between his legs.

Her palms made contact with the center of his back and she stepped into his body. Her breasts were soft and pliant, her belly a sweet curve beneath his backside. He didn't think she could possibly get any closer but, when her cheek came to rest on his spine, she proved him wrong.

He spread his free hand over his abs and then slid his fingers to the base of his cock where he pressed hard to stop the pulse of semen ready to flow. Not yet, not so soon, not when they hadn't yet tasted heaven or one another.

Erin nuzzled her face against him, moved her hands to his shoulders, slid her palms the length of his arms, stopping only when her one hand reached his holding his erection. She worked her fingers underneath his palm and silently demanded he show her the way he liked to be stroked.

If her touch wouldn't have guaranteed an abrupt end to their shared pleasure, he would have gladly spread his legs and let her have her way. Instead, he cupped her hand over the head of his cock, thrust once, oh, damn, into her hand. Then, shaking, he turned.

Her beauty caught him with a sharp sucker punch. Water streamed down her face, through lashes matted together over huge hazel eyes. Her nose was a perky button, her mouth wide and lush and the dream of a man and his dick.

He couldn't wait to see her come again. To see her eyes flash and her nostrils flare and hear sounds she had no reason to hold back. Moving his hands to her shoulders, he backed her across the enclosure until her heels hit the base of the bench built into the wall. He wanted her to sit, to spread her legs and feed his hunger.

He wanted to give her pleasure more than he remembered caring to share with any other woman. And a part of him realized he was feeling that desire in more places than those so obviously physical and that made absolutely no sense. He shoved the thoughts away and bent to taste the skin along her jawline, his hands at her rib cage, his thumbs pressing into the plump sides of her breasts.

Her skin tasted like the sea, and she had the most gorgeous breasts, tipped with hard, dark cherry centers. Leaving tiny nips the length of her neck to her shoulder, he leaned down and sucked a nipple into his mouth. She gasped at first and then she moaned, her fingers digging into his biceps as she held on to him for support.

He slid his hands from her shoulders to her elbows, pinning her arms to her sides and urging her down to the bench built into the wall. She went without question. Sebastian followed, dropping to his knees between her legs. He glanced up and, in the swirling steam, he saw her eyes blaze.

Her expression kicked him in the gut. The heady mix of desire and uncertain anticipation would've been enough to make him rethink what they were doing if he'd been capable of anything resembling thought. As it was, he was nothing but a creature of appetite and a man's most elemental focus. This moment meant nothing but her pleasure. He lifted her legs, draped her knees over his shoulders.

And then he moved his mouth to her sex.

At the first touch from the tip of his tongue, she cried out. And shuddered. He felt her tremors where his hands held her inner thighs, his thumbs pressed to her flesh so soft and firm and giving. He loved a woman's skin. He loved this one's taste. She brought to mind grapefruit, and olives, a salty sweetness warmed by her body's heat and that of the water raining down.

He moved his hands closer to the creases where hips met thighs and slid his thumbs into the folds of her sex, pulling her open to expose her swollen clit and the slick opening to her pussy, a slickness that had nothing to do with the water beating down and everything to do with carnality and lust.

His kissed her, his mouth open on her sex, so plump and ripe and his balls drew up hard, his cock surging up toward his belly. He wanted to wrap his hand around his shaft and watch himself enter her body. That first thrust, the thought of being inside this woman... He shuddered and entered her with his tongue.

She gasped and arched against him, her hands braced at her hips holding her weight. She pulled her knees to her chest, moved her feet to his shoulders for leverage. Her eager response totally did him in. His tongue circled her clit. He sucked it into his mouth while he fingered her to the same rhythm his other hand used to stroke his cock.

Nothing in his memory, hell, nothing in his imagination had ever been this sharp, this intense, this ball-bustingly hot. He was going to come and that's all there was to it. He had Erin Thatcher in his shower, her legs spread and his body screaming with weeks worth of pent-up want. He wanted to pull her down onto his lap and let her ride him hard. But he was so close and the thought of stopping for a condom was a killer.

It was only when he felt her fingers come to rest on his that he opened his eyes to realize that, some time during his fantasy, he'd abandoned the real Erin for the imagined. He had to be out of his mind. Reaching for the fictional when he had the real thing. Her feet now rested on his thighs and he didn't even remember letting her go.

He looked up, caught off guard by the tongue she held to the bow of her upper lip while she watched him jerk off. Her fingers slid over his to the head of his dick then she pulled her heels up onto the bench and sat, knees up and separated, exposing herself completely.

And then she slipped her own hand between her legs, her own finger into her sex. He couldn't believe what he was seeing. This wasn't at all what he had planned but damn if he could find a reason to stop her. Or to stop himself. Especially when she met his gaze directly and said, ''I want to watch you come.''

He got to his feet then, a move that put his crotch in her direct line of vision. And then he began to stroke in earnest, rubbing the flat of his palm up and over the head and back down the shaft. He pumped harder, his gaze flicking from her fascinated expression to her own sweet sex that she fingered.

He wanted to be everywhere at once, in her sex, her hands, her mouth, her tight little…oh, fuck. He groaned and let go, shooting semen into the swirl of foggy air, working his cock, pumping, stroking, until he was spent. Spent but still amazingly hard. An anomaly of which Erin took notice.

He sank onto the bench opposite the one where she sat. Though she didn't sit long, pushing up to her feet and crossing the enclosure to stand before him. He expected her to drop to her knees. Instead, she reached above him for a cloth and the bottles of shampoo and bath soap he kept there on a shelf. She set soap and cloth on the bench beneath the center showerhead and set about washing her hair.

Sebastian found himself transfixed. He couldn't tear his gaze away from the picture of Erin's hands in her hair, her eyes closed, her chin up as the spray pelted her face, sending the suds streaming down her spine and over the sweet curve of her backside.

When she reached for the liquid soap and the cloth, he felt the first new stirrings of desire in his gut. He snorted to himself. What a lie. Desire hadn't laid down once since the birth of this obsession. The proof was in his erection that remained at half mast.

And now, with Erin sliding that soapy cloth over her shoulders, down her arms to her elbows to her wrists, and even her fingers, his fixation sharpened.

She moved the cloth to her throat, across her collarbone and down over her breasts, cupping them as she washed the full swells and gumdrop nipples. She stood in profile and suds slid down her limbs, pooling at her feet, her body slick and gleaming.

His hard-on stiffened further, straining toward his belly and begging to be stroked. He refused, and he waited, feeling strangled as he sat unmoving, strangled, tied in knots, grabbed hard by body parts better left unbound.

But when she moved the cloth to soap her inner thighs, bringing the fabric and her hands up between her legs and turning to face him, meeting his gaze directly and putting on a show mortal man had never been meant to resist, Sebastian succumbed to human nature and the call of the wild.

He grabbed up a condom from where the stack Erin had brought into the shower had fallen to the floor and, in three quick strides he was there, and the suds soaping her skin provided an intoxicating friction when he wrapped his arms around her body and backed her into the wall.

Her breath whooshed out from the force of his motion. He told himself to back off, back down and be gentle. But then she dug her fingertips into his shoulders and worked her heels into the backs of his thighs, levering herself up between his body and the wall.

He slid a forearm beneath her for support then tipped his lower body toward her. She released her hold on his shoulder with one hand and reached between their bodies for his cock, guiding him to the opening of her sex and, even after he thrust upward, after he buried himself in her warmth and she gasped, she kept her fingers wrapped around the base of his shaft.

The pressure she applied would've made for a damn

good cock ring but it was *her* hand and not a strip of leather or a metal circle and that made all the difference in the feelings surging through him. He shoved hard against her. It was all he could do. He had no room to withdraw, to feel the head of his cock breach her opening the way he wanted. Again and again.

To feel that first pressing thrust, that push of flesh on flesh, firm into supple, insistent into giving, his hard-as-a-wooden-bat erection buried in the rich complement of her glove soft sex. She ground down against him, squeezing him with inner muscles and that one friggin' hand.

That was it. He grabbed her ass with both hands, pressed his chest into her chest for support as he drove himself into her body and exploded. Erin whimpered, both hands now clutching his shoulders, moving down his back, clawing and scratching as she tried to pull him farther inside to assuage her arousal's itch and ache.

When she came her spasms rocked the both of them. She cried out, and would've fallen if he hadn't braced her up, leaned against her, kept her safe. He felt her contractions grip and pull him farther inside and he shook from the force of her body's response. She shook as well, her head back, her back arched, her hands slapped flat to the wall. Her climax nearly brought him to his knees.

When the force of her completion subsided, when her strength was taxed and her energy spent, he sank to the enclosure's floor, still holding her tight, still buried deep inside. She curled arms and legs around him and he couldn't tell where he started, where she began.

The water continued to beat down. The steam continued to swirl and rise. Sebastian leaned back against the base of the bench, wrapped both arms around Erin where she sat in his lap, and did his best to breathe.

He'd just compromised the entire reason he'd had this shower built. Solitude, personal safety, peace of mind. He'd never step inside again without thinking of Erin in his arms.

And he wasn't at all sure he was comfortable with that.

5

CALI GLANCED AT HER WATCH, shook her head, blinked away the grit from her tired eyes—grit leftover from work and Thursday's makeup she'd never washed away—and glanced at her watch one more time. Unbelievable. She'd never even made it home from work and now she was due in class in thirty minutes.

Last night after leaving Paddington's, she'd joined Will at IHOP for a middle of the night brainstorming session over Cherry Coke and French fries. Both had been too wound up for sleep and agreed the time would be well spent in working through their screenplay's plot elements.

For hours they'd played "what if," scratching notes as they challenged one another to up the stakes in their collaborative story's twists and turns, to dig for deeper motivation, to breathe life into their characters with added details of personality and goals…and to work on ways to increase the internal conflict between their two main protagonists, not to mention giving the antagonist a better developed back story of his own.

Half the night Cali found herself wondering when Will had become so hardheaded, and if they'd ever come to a meeting of the minds.

Toward that end, they'd stayed until the smell of maple syrup, sausage and hot-buttered pancakes had roused their stomachs for breakfast. Hot coffee had accompanied the meal and given them both a second wind. Had that really been two hours ago? Double unbelievable. She blew out an aggravated breath, shoving a hand back through her hair.

Now she was going to have to skip all the errands she'd planned to run this one free afternoon of the week and catch a nap between class and tonight's shift at work. If not, she'd crash and burn big time. And she *so* did not want to piss off Erin by dragging ass on a Friday night.

Cali gathered her things, shoving pencils, spiral bound and colored index cards, a letter-size legal pad and a textbook into her tote bag, then dug out her wallet to pay for her share of the shared meals.

Will stopped her with a warm hand covering hers. "What're you doing?"

"It's seven-thirty. I have class at eight on Friday." She pointed to her watch. It was now, actually, seven thirty-five. Even worse. "I'm never going to make it."

"You've been late to class before."

"I know, but I hate being late. And skipping is just so not me. I've paid out all this tuition and missing a lecture means I'm not getting my money's worth." Besides, she had to look like crap, being up all night. Baggy raccoon eyes. Splotchy skin. Frizzed out curls from too much tearing out of her hair.

And then there was the little tiny issue of realizing how comfortably intimate the night had been without anything physical going on when she'd actually been thinking of inviting Will to her bed. How could she risk screwing things up for the sake of sex? Sex that she could find elsewhere. Except she didn't want sex elsewhere.

She wanted sex with Will.

"What if I make you a better offer?"

Her head came up from where she'd been looking through her tote for her car keys. Will's eyes were bright, his gaze teasing but issuing a challenge that hit her hard enough to knock the air from her lungs.

She huffed out what breath she had left in response. "What could possibly be better than listening to Professor Smith yammer on about genre fiction?"

"A nap." Will shoved his open legal pad into his satchel, dropped his number two yellow pencil in beside and stuffed his textbook into the remaining space. He wore a distracted look while packing up his things and Cali wondered if he was even aware of what he'd said.

She wondered even more exactly what he'd meant. "You want to take a nap?"

Will looked up, dragged a hand down his face. Then he grinned, a lopsided boyish expression that added a twinkle to his eyes. "That didn't come out exactly the way I'd planned, did it? God, I'm exhausted."

Exactly what she'd been afraid of, she thought, and sighed. Good thing she knew him well enough not to feel slighted that he'd taken back an offer when he really hadn't made one at all. "That's what you get for being a talk, talk, thinker. The worst open-mouth, insert-foot type I've ever seen."

Will grinned widely, crossing forearms and bracing elbows on the table to lean closer toward where she sat in the opposite booth. "I like to speak my mind and, yeah, it gets me in more than a little bit of trouble. But it also ends up getting me what I want."

"Like a nap?" she asked, brows arched. She really did need to get moving. At least the part of her devoted to her degree in creative writing. But the other part of her, the part devoted more to Will—even if it was a borderline schoolgirl devotion—wanted to stay and listen to him worm his way out of the nap he'd offered.

He seemed to ponder the idea, taking his time coming to a decision, the same time she was wasting. One of them had to make a move and, as much as she longed to spend her time enjoying his company, her education called. She hoisted the strap of her tote bag over her shoulder…

…at the same time Will slapped his hands on the table. "Let's do it. Why not. You can read Professor Smith's lecture online this weekend. You know she'll have it uploaded by this afternoon. Her ego will allow for no less."

Cali hesitated. If she left now, she'd miss maybe fifteen minutes of class, barring no run-ins with rush-hour traffic. Who was she kidding? This was Houston, Texas. Have car, will drive everywhere.

She might as well follow Will's example and catch up on her sleep. Sleep, right. She *so* could not believe she was this easy, jumping when he hadn't even snapped his fingers. What had happened to her spine?

"So, we nap. Then what? You want to meet for lunch and see if we can come to an agreement on this third turning point?" She turned her aggravation with herself back to her aggravation with their number one screenplay issue of the moment. She narrowed her gaze and drilled him hard. "Or do you just want to admit now that I'm right and there's no way Jason can go back to the boat dock and risk being caught?"

"You're so far off base, Cali. If Jason doesn't find the knife at the dock, he can't be connected to the fire." Will frowned. "I thought we already settled this."

"No, you settled what *you* think should happen.

You're back to thinking plot, not character, and that just won't work in this case. This turning point has to be all about Jason's need to prove his innocence.'' Cali got to her feet, tossed down her half of the food bill and an extra large tip. She knew all about working for tips.

Will followed suit, thumbing through his billfold and hesitating longer than Cali had over how much extra to leave. She glanced up, caught the wry twist to his mouth and said, ''We've been here all night and poor Dora has been a total doll to take care of us. Don't be a cheapskate.''

''Ordinarily, I wouldn't be.'' He added a handful of bills to the ones on the table and shrugged, stuffing his wallet down in his back pocket. ''But as of yesterday I'm unemployed and not likely to find another agency as flexible as Kirkwood's was.''

Will had done freelance graphics work for the advertising firm as long as Cali had known him. Shocked wasn't even the word for what she felt. She hardly knew what to say. ''They let you go? Just like that? Why didn't you tell me?''

Oh, God, she felt all sorts of caregiver instincts kick in, when more than anything Will would be needing a friend.

''I did tell you. Just now.'' He put his hand in the small of her back and headed them toward the door. ''And, yeah. They let me go. Business is slow. Not much reason to keep me around and pay me for doing nothing but looking good.''

''What are you going to do?'' And why did she feel the sudden urge to invite him to move in to her place and share expenses? She couldn't even find a response to his comment about looking good.

"Right now I'm going to take a nap." They'd reached their cars parked side by side. The rising sun had Will squinting and replacing his glasses with the prescription sunshades from the case shoved down in the pocket of his baggy khaki Dockers. "You going to follow me? Or you just want to hitch a ride? I can bring you back to get your car later, if you want."

What was he talking about, hitching a ride? Following? Bringing her back to get her car later? Her heart pattered like a thunderstorm on glass. He wanted them to nap together? Oh, great. Now she couldn't breathe. The only safe thing she could think of to say was, "I thought you wanted to meet for lunch later?"

"I'll fix us lunch." He unlocked and opened the door to his sporty black Eclipse. "I'll dig out a pair of sweats and a T-shirt. You can shower then sleep on the futon in the living room."

"The futon. Perfect." Sleeping on his furniture wearing his clothes. Naked in his shower while he…did what? Went about his business as if she wasn't naked in his shower, waiting to put on his clothes and sleep on his furniture? "I'll follow you. I'll need my car later and it'll be out of the way to come back and pick it up here."

"Great. I figure by noon we should be human again. And then you'll see that it only makes sense for Jason to find the knife at the dock." Will dropped down into the driver's seat and slammed the door, giving her a thumbs-up as the engine raced to life.

God, but he was such a guy! Playful and sexy and he made her laugh and caused her tummy to tingle and she loved arguing with him over their screenplay ideas and oh, but she was afraid she was getting close to falling in love.

She stuck out her tongue in a teasing response, and then she tossed her things into her own car's passenger seat, backed out the candy apple red Focus and pulled behind Will into the traffic that wasn't quite as heavy as she'd expected this hour of the morning.

She'd been to his apartment more than once, an apartment that was actually the second floor of an old Victorian house close to downtown, but always to work on their project. He'd cooked dinner a couple of times early in the semester and they'd sat at his kitchen table to hash out their story ideas. True, it didn't happen often because of the very schedules they'd bemoaned last night.

So why was she getting her hopes up that today was going to be any different? He hadn't invited her over as a date—since they weren't *dating,* only hanging out like they'd decided yesterday—but as his study partner. She'd kissed his cheek and that was it. Now they were both going to sleep. So what? They weren't going to be sleeping together. And that pretty much answered her question about the future of their relationship.

Or the nonfuture of our nonrelationship, she grumped to herself, turning up the volume on Alanis Morissette and belting out her irritation under the guise of singing along. And, why not? She sure didn't have a Man To Do to help her work off the frustration. Lucky Erin.

ERIN AND SEBASTIAN NEVER made it out of the shower. Hours later and she still couldn't believe it. She'd been a wrung-out, wrinkled prune by the time she'd dried off and dressed and backed her way through Sebastian's loft—hard to do when he'd followed her, dripping and naked and once again hard—from the bathroom to the front door.

Once there, he'd braced a hand above her shoulder and leaned toward her, smelling of warm clean skin and fresh sex. He'd buried his face in her neck and taken her hand in his, wrapping their joined fingers around his erection and stroking in that rhythm she now knew so well.

He'd opened the door before he'd come. She'd ducked through with a wordless goodbye, stood on the other side and listened to his labored groans, his grunts, the strangled agony of a man in pain—or pleasure. She wondered if he knew she'd waited. She wondered why she had. Even then, as she'd found herself waiting, seeking signs of his movement, his breathing, his heartbeat through the solid wooden door...even then, she'd wondered why she'd stayed. Finally, she'd had to go.

She'd hurried back to her own place, the sounds of Sebastian's struggle still ringing in her ears and her body responding to that need he hadn't shared. During none of the times they'd come together, or the times they'd gotten one another off, had Erin sensed his release to be as rich as the completion he'd found there alone behind his closed door.

If he did know that she'd waited, she wanted to know what he'd thought, how he'd felt about her remaining until he'd finished. She still hadn't decided why she'd stayed. Except that so many things about Sebastian Gallo intrigued her. The size of his library and the opulence of his shower just to name two.

After all that time they'd spent wrapped up in the steam and the spray, she'd known if she'd gone anywhere near his bed she wouldn't have wanted to leave. Neither would she have wanted to sleep and she was desperately exhausted, not to mention achy and sore and more than a little bit raw. Tomorrow she had a meeting with the caterer to finalize the menu for the Halloween anniversary bash. And she needed sleep.

She'd had her pleasure. Hell, in one night she'd had pleasures she'd been without for months, if not all of her life. Now that she was home, it was back to whatever business she could manage before tumbling into bed. At least until the next time Sebastian crooked his finger. And after doing the one thing she had to do before crawling between the sheets.

Call Cali.

A call to her cell produced, "The customer you are trying to reach is unavailable," which meant Cali had forgotten again to turn on her phone. And a call to her home phone got voice mail. Desperate enough to page her, Erin glanced at her bedside clock while kicking off her shoes.

Well, duh. Cali would be on her way to her Friday morning class and wouldn't be home before Erin was asleep. That left one option. E-mail her Men To Do girlfriends. She stripped off her clothes for the second time tonight, and swore she could still smell Sebastian on her skin.

She tugged her nightshirt over her head and settled down into her pillows, settling her laptop on a pillow in her lap.

From: Erin Thatcher
Sent: Friday
To: Samantha Tyler; Tess Norton
Subject: My Scary Guy

I did it! Er, him. I did him! I can't believe it! He was absolutely amazing. And, no, not Hannibal Lecter scary at all, though he is definitely frightening in an intimidatingly sexy sort of way.

I had no idea there were actually men who knew how to do the things he did. My body is still reeling. I SO totally picked the right Man To Do! I'd share the juicy details but I'm too exhausted to type, much less figure out how to put thoughts into words.

Which brings me to my problem. I'm not supposed to be thinking about this, am I? This is supposed to be all about sex, right? So, why am I dying to get to know him? Is this that female thing in action? Where we can't separate the physical from the emotional? I don't want the bloody emotional! I don't want anything but the physical. Period. End of story.

But I do want to know why he has a shower that belongs in a locker room. No, not a locker room. More like a hedonistic resort. We're talking three showerheads and staggered levels of built-in benches perfect for, well, yeah, that. And more of that. At least two hours of that. I'm not kidding. I'm a total prune. And I may never walk again!

He also has a virtual library in his living room. The rolling ladder and everything. No television. Just a high-tech sound system like you wouldn't believe and books that go on forever. Classics and bestsellers and psychology texts and…the list goes on.

It's like, if I were looking for a relationship, I'd say he has more potential than any man I've known in ages. I feel like I ought to give it a go, just in case.

What if he turned out to be The One? But I'm just not ready. So what do I do? Besides whine!

Oh, and his name is Sebastian Gallo. Love, Erin

She didn't bother to proofread. She was way past exhausted and figured even the most glaring mistakes would get by her foggy, bleary eyes. She hit Send then moved her laptop to the bedside table, leaving the connection open, thinking maybe Tess would check her e-mail before heading out to wave her green-thumb wand over the houseplants of Manhattan.

Or maybe Samantha wouldn't have a client meeting or a court date this early and could whip out a quick reply to help Erin make sense of the night. She felt fuzzy-headed and goofy. And wrung-out and giggly and on the verge of tears. All the symptoms of a classic sex hangover. And what a doozy.

But as appealing as she found the idea of returning upstairs for the hair of the dog that bit her, and bit her, and bit her again, she couldn't think straight about anything without at least a few hours of sleep.

And tomorrow was Friday, ugh, *today* was Friday, one of her busiest weeknights. Figures that she'd start the affair she'd been dying to engage in when she didn't have time to enjoy it. But when *would* she have time to enjoy it? It wasn't like tomorrow was going to be any less stressful than today.

And the day after would be even worse being Sunday—the only day of the week she had time to take care of personal business, though lately the only thing personal she did was go to church and buy tampons. Oh, and catch up on her much needed sleep.

The remainder of her time was devoted to the business of Paddington's. The business of keeping Paddington's alive for her own sake since it was her sole means of income. But also keeping the bar viable for Rory.

Rory who wasn't here, who would never be here again to tuck her under his wing, to encourage her to keep her chin up, or to praise the work she'd done to his place. No. *Her* place, damn it. It was her place. Why was she having so much trouble seeing things that way?

Perhaps because more than anything else, he would never be here to forgive her for getting the hell out of Dodge the minute she'd received her inheritance at age eighteen. For putting her degree on the back burner next to his advice that she not blow the money her parents had intended for her education.

Or for taking such little interest in a place that meant so much to him that, after moving to Texas to raise her, he'd worked the rest of his life duplicating his Devonshire pub only to have her turn it into what she wanted it to be the minute he was gone. She was some piece of work, wasn't she?

Before Erin took that thought beyond her comfort zone, the chime of her e-mail bell sounded. She leaned over and clicked it open to read.

From: Tess Norton
Sent: Friday
To: Erin Thatcher; Samantha Tyler
Subject: Re: My Scary Guy

You bitch! (Oops, did I say that out loud? I meant, wow, how fabulous for you!!!) I mean it, girl. This is outstanding. I have no good advice, however. I suck at this relationship thing, remember? But I do think the way to approach this whole business is to do what feels right, even if it feels scary. Maybe because it feels scary.

It's all a crap shoot, dear Erin, didn't you know that? And the dice don't give a damn if you think you're ready or not. So you might as well have fun as long as you're already in the game.

Perhaps lots and lots more sex will make things clearer. And if it doesn't, you'll be too tired to care. Love and kisses, Tess

Ha! Tess was just way too upbeat this morning, damn the woman. If sex made things clearer, why this horribly muddled state of mind? She was right about the exhaustion level, however. At least about it existing. Erin felt like she would need the jaws of life to pry her body out of this bed.

Now if she could only get to that place where she was too tired to care. Or at least too tired to think about caring. Too tired to think, period, sounded even better. Though dreaming about Sebastian sounded like an excellent plan. And she was drifting off to do just that when her e-mail chime sounded again. She propped up on one elbow to read.

From: Samantha Tyler
Sent: Friday
To: Erin Thatcher; Tess Norton
Subject: Re: My Scary Guy

Oh, Erin. So many responses! And I'm having a hard time separating all my personal divorce baggage from what a true friend would say so bear with me.

First of all, YUM on the sex. If I wasn't sure I'd freak, I'd be asking if Sebastian (such a cool name!)

had any brothers. In the meantime, I'm way happy for you. You deserve every orgasm and bowlegged morning-after you get. Whew! (fanning self)

Second, oh God, be careful. Having sex with a scary guy is scary enough, but feelings? Weren't those entirely outside of the point of Men To Do? They were, you know it.

I guess I'd say follow your instincts. You're not some dopey bimbo, so you know you won't get in deep if he's really no good. But be careful, careful and more careful. Men give their gender a bad name.

Cheers and a victory salute, Samantha

Erin smiled. No, she was not a dopey bimbo, she mused, disconnecting from her ISP. Samantha and Tess were the absolute best. Erin's cyber buddies had provided the perfect sleep tonic to ease her mind, and given her the food for thought she needed to hold her until later tonight.

Then she'd get Cali to talk her back to sanity.

A NIGGLING LITTLE ITCH brought Cali from deep sleep to the edge of wakefulness. She snuggled her face into her pillow, pulling her sheet and thick duvet to her chin.

But this wasn't her pillow, she thought, eyes closed and frowning as consciousness began to return. And this wasn't her duvet or sheet but a worn quilt that felt like the softest cotton on her skin. At least the skin exposed and not covered by the unfamiliar sleepwear...

Will's T-shirt and sweats. Will's quilt and Will's pillow. She smiled, rubbed the fabric to her cheek. If this was his idea of hanging out, she was definitely in for a pound. She couldn't remember the last time she'd been this comfortable sleeping in her own bed.

Which was silly, because she loved her bed. But sleeping here, in Will's place, in his clothes, on his futon, beneath his quilt? She snuggled deeper into the pillow. It was as if she was surrounded by the one thing her life was lacking and she most wanted to find.

Funny, because she truly thought herself happy and fulfilled. And she was happy and fulfilled. Life was great, what with her job and her classes and that disastrous relationship nightmare behind her...

She found herself frowning again and this time opened her eyes, closed them, opened them again and blinked hard. Her heart dropped from her throat, where it beat like a wild butterfly's wings, to her stomach. Will was lying beside her, facing her, his eyes looking straight into hers as she came fully awake.

She curled her body into a tighter ball, keeping the butterfly close. "What're you doing here?"

He grinned his Cheshire cat grin. "I live here."

The purr of his words vibrated the length of her spine. "I know that part. I meant why aren't you in your bed? Couldn't you sleep?"

"I slept. A couple of hours worth." His face was so close she could see new tiny gold whiskers above the scruffy five o'clock shadow he never completely shaved.

She could see the darker flecks in his light brown eyes, and the two or three wild hairs growing straight up out of his eyebrows. He wore glasses most all of the time and she'd never been so close to his eyes. Or to the rest of his body that, oh, God, she hoped wasn't as naked.

Her eyes widened, and she glanced down briefly to see what he was wearing. Not a lot. Nothing but a pair of gray jersey gym shorts. Her heart began to thump harder.

Catching at her bottom lip with her teeth, she moved her gaze back to his, hoping against hope that she sounded calmer than she felt with cocoons bursting open in her belly. "How do you expect to make it through the day on two hours of sleep?"

His arms crossed over his chest, his hands tucked into his armpits, he shrugged the shoulder he wasn't lying on. "I'm young, hale and hearty. I'll live."

He was so blasé. How could he be so blasé when her entire body flinched every time his long lashes blinked? "How long have you been looking at me?"

This time he hesitated before answering, taking his time with the words as if they mattered more than those he'd spoken before. One corner of his mouth lifted and softly he said, "For at least two months now."

"No. I mean…" She stopped, stunned. *Two months?* That meant he'd been looking at her since they'd met at the beginning of the fall semester. He couldn't mean… When all this time… And now he was looking at her… "I mean how long—"

Will shifted up onto his elbows and leaned over her, his face but inches away. "Cali."

Cali rolled onto her back, deciding this wasn't going to be about napping and hanging out after all. She could only manage to whisper her answer. "Will?"

He reached out and twirled one of her wild blond

curls around his index finger. "Last night. In Paddington's. We talked about spending time together. Hanging out and having fun. Not messing with the screenplay. Not trying to talk while you work. Do you remember that?"

She nodded. Did he really think she'd forget?

"What happened next?"

She didn't even pretend not to know what he was talking about. "I kissed you."

"Yep." Will pulled his finger from her curl to touch it to the bow of her upper lip. "Did you know I couldn't make a single note that made sense after that?"

No. She didn't know that at all. But she wasn't about to feign disappointment, because that was the moment anticipation struck with a vengeance, sweeping through her belly and down between her legs. "Why?"

"Because you walked away too soon. And I wanted more than anything to kiss you back."

She eased her grip on the quilt and pushed it to her waist. She wanted to be as close to him as she possibly could because she'd been ready for this forever. "Will?"

His fingertips traced the whole of her mouth and moved to her chin. "Cali?"

She lifted a hand to the round of his bare shoulder. "You can kiss me now."

His smile before he lowered his head nearly broke her heart. He brushed his lips oh, so lightly over hers, mouths closed and barely touching as they shared the air they both breathed.

He shifted even closer, his bare chest brushing across her aroused nipples beneath the cotton of his shirt that she wore. The pressure increased, his mouth and his body and the ache buried deep in her core. She wanted him like no man she'd ever wanted. And she told him so when she opened her mouth, asking him to open his in return.

He did and tongues tangled and teethed clashed and hands explored exposed skin and roughly shed clothes to bare more, to bare everything. His body was glorious, smooth and firm where her hands ran over his shoulders and back and buttocks.

He shifted slightly, allowing room for her discovery to move where he most wanted her touch. Sliding her hand down his flat belly, she wrapped her hand around him, so hard, so satiny soft, and she shivered.

He gasped and he groaned. "Cali, you're making me crazy."

Crazy was a good thing, yes? Because, if not, this insanity would bring big fat regrets once they came to their senses. She stroked him again, running her palm up and over the head of his penis, so huge and so swollen. "This is good, then? I don't want to do it wrong."

He gave a strangled laugh. "Nothing you could do would be wrong. Trust me on this."

He thrust into her hand. And this time *she* gasped, imagining that thrust taking him into her body. Yet that gasp became nothing when Will moved down her body and ran the flat of his tongue across the hard peak of her breast. He kiss-nipped the plump flesh before centering his attention on her nipple that begged.

"Oh, Will," was all she could say because now his fingers were slipping between her legs, slipping through the wet folds of her sex, slipping into her body that wept with wanting. She arched her hips into his hand and cried out.

His fingers delved deeper, stroking, rubbing, his thumb teasing her clit that throbbed with the need to come. She didn't want to come without him. Not this first perfect time. This time she wanted to come to the filling drive of his sex and the pressing weight of his body covering hers. "Will, please."

"Please what, Cali?" he asked, sliding back up to kiss the underside of her jaw, her ear, her neck where it met her shoulder.

She could hardly find the words for what she wanted. And her whisper shook. "Please, please me. I want you to fill me. I want you inside of me. I want—"

"Every damn thing that I want." He braced his weight on his elbows, slid his arms beneath her shoulders and cupped the back of her head. "Cali, honey. You have no idea how much I've wanted to do this and for how long."

When he kissed her this time their mouths came together in a sweet expression of tender feelings, feelings new and unexpected and frightening in that way of a journey into the unknown. When he moved his hand to caress her breast, sensation heightened to a singing pitch of expectation, anticipation, a sharp, fevered want.

When he deftly moved to ensure her protection, when he urged her legs open and settled his weight in her body's cradle, when he guided his sheathed erection to the waiting center of her sex, Cali knew no moment in her life would ever again be this perfect.

At Will's first probing test of her readiness, she caught back a cry of emotion that quickly became a long sigh of nothing but relief at finally, finally, oh, finally he was there, inside her, his first beautiful thrust filling her and she shuddered and he stopped and he groaned, a sound that came from deep in his gut and was so much a part of what she was feeling she barely managed to breathe.

But she didn't want him to stop and she urged him to move with the fingers she gouged into his backside and *oh, yes,* that was where she wanted him, right there where she was so tightly wound up, pressing, grinding, *there, that's it, oh, no, no, not so soon.* She wasn't ready to come, wasn't ready, didn't want, no, this first time, not so fast…as if she could put a halt to what Will had started when she'd first opened her eyes and seen him lying beside her.

"Will, I can't wait. I want to wait." She panted sharply. "I want to wait."

"'s okay, baby." He sounded as out of control as she was. "Next time. We'll do this slow and easy next time."

Next time? He wanted her again. He wanted her again. She didn't even know how she would survive the here and now. "Are you sure?"

He panted to a stop. "The only thing I'm sure about is that this has to happen now."

And then he surged upward, his back bowing as he drove into her body. Cali let go and the thrilling burst that followed took her higher than she'd known she could go. Will's thrusts remained constant and steady, the pressure perfect, the position exactly right and she shivered and trembled until her focus eased away from the sensation between her legs to take in the sensation of Will.

Cali smiled. He'd waited for her. He'd waited, making sure she found heaven in her release. She felt the taut restraint in the muscles of his shoulders and back and moved her hands to his backside that was equally tight. She dug her fingers into his buttocks, her heels into the backs of his thighs and rolled up against him.

He buried his face in the crease where her neck met her shoulder and growled. The tempo of his movements increased at her urging. She met his every downward thrust with a hard upward arch of her lower body until she sensed he was on the verge of losing control.

When he came he would've driven Cali off the end of the futon and into the wall if not for the buttress of pillows. He shook, shuddered, his entire body racked by a completion so powerful Cali found herself fighting back tears—and wondering if he'd been waiting for her as long as she'd been for him.

6

When Cali burst through the door of the Paddington's office thirty minutes before she was due to clock in for her Friday night shift, Erin looked up from the shuffle of paperwork spread across her desk. The caterer had just left after spending two hours finalizing the menu for the party, yet Erin still wasn't sure the choices she'd made were the best.

She was sure, however, that Cali was about to pop. Erin didn't know if she would do better to come right out and ask, or to let Cali blurt it out when she was ready. What Erin did instead was broach the subject forefront in her mind. "Have you seen the rerun of *Seinfeld* where Jerry eats the black and white cookie then throws up for the first time in years?"

Cali plopped down in the only extra chair in the office, a thrift-store number with crushed velvet gold cushions and freshly varnished arms and legs, and shoved her backpack up underneath. "I think so. Where he and Elaine are in the bakery to pick up a babka and she finds a hair? Why?"

Erin nodded. "That's the one. And I'm only asking because the caterer has black and white cookies on the menu and I wonder if that's what everyone at the party is going to be thinking about. Jerry Seinfeld vomiting."

Cali shrugged and tucked her crossed legs up into

the chair. ''So what if they are? It'll add some appropriate Halloween gore.''

''I don't know.'' Erin shook her head slowly while she thought. ''I just think it has a huge potential ick factor, don't you?''

Cali nodded toward the papers on Erin's desk. ''What else is on the menu?''

Erin put the pages of the proposal back into order. ''Don't forget, I had to take into consideration a mingling crowd and limited seats, so I did what I could to minimize the need for utensils.''

''Finger foods.''

''For the most part.'' The look of concern, no, the look of disgust on Cali's face gave Erin pause. ''You don't think that's a problem, do you? I mean, it's not like we're a full service restaurant here to begin with. The caterer is the one putting things together.''

A set of blond brows lifted. ''Do you have booze?''

''Uh, hello? This is a bar.''

Cali waved a dismissive hand. ''Then anything works.''

''Okay, then,'' Erin said, deciding Cali's attitude better be about whatever had brought her flying in here or she was going to find herself smacked back to reality. ''We have black grapes and white pears. Black bean soup with white rice. Peppered roast beef on white bread. Turkey breast on pumpernickel—''

''So far, so good.'' Cali held up a finger. ''But I'll be heading straight for the chocolate, which you had better have in horrific quantities.''

''Trust me. There will be trays of white, milk and dark chocolate truffles everywhere.'' And she would be the next in line behind Cali. Erin flipped to the second page of the proposed menu.

"Also, toasted marshmallows and chocolate fondue, which works for the fruit, too. Then the obvious devil's food cake and angel food cake. The black and white cookies…maybe. Chocolate mousse brownies and almond blancmange. White and Black Russians. White grape and blackberry punch."

"Spiked?"

"Of course." And that was it. She stacked the pages and waited for Cali's reaction. "So, what do you think?"

Heaving a sigh, Cali slumped down to sit on her spine in the chair. "The only thing I can think about right now is the morning I spent in bed with Will."

Erin blinked, blinked again, shook off her shock and almost shouted, "You did what?"

"I know, can you believe it?"

"No. I can't believe it. You were just whining yesterday about not wanting to screw up your friendship with Will."

"I know. This was just one of those spontaneous things and I didn't have time to think."

"Or maybe this was your subconscious's way of telling you to quit thinking. You've really been obsessing over this way too much, you know."

"I know, I know. Now all I can do is wait and see what happens." Cali blew out a long slow sigh. "I had no idea sex could be so invigorating and exhausting at the same time. Well, I mean I knew about the exhausting part but usually that's more a case of being too tired to even make an effort at orgasm."

Erin chuckled. The old cliché of "Been there, done that" seemed to fit. "And this time?"

Head plopped against the chair back, Cali closed her

eyes. "This time is definitely a case of being exhausted from the orgasms."

"A sex hangover. I know."

One Cali eye opened. "You, too?"

Erin nodded. "Sebastian. His name is Sebastian."

Cali's second eye opened. Her head came up. "Is that his real name or his Scary Guy name?"

"Funny," Erin said, even as she tried not to laugh. "It would be a good Scary Guy name, wouldn't it?"

"What's his last name?"

"Gallo. Sebastian Gallo."

"Oh, that's even better," Cali scoffed. "Gallo? As in, 'Get a rope'?"

"I don't know about the gallows part—" Erin's mouth twisted. She really couldn't help herself. "—but he's certainly hung."

"Eww. Too much information, Erin. Feel free to keep that to yourself." Cali paused, then lost the battle with her own prurient grin. "Though, I must say that Will is certainly not lacking in that, uh, area either."

Frowning, Erin tapped the end of her pencil against the desktop. "Do you think guys really have size issues?"

"Not as much as we do, worrying about our own butts and boobs. Actually, I think once they have us naked and writhing they're more worried they might leave us hanging. And I don't mean that gallows thing you were just bragging about."

Erin sighed. Then Cali sighed. Both slumped back in their respective chairs and took a long, daydreaming moment. Erin had a feeling her best friend was no more in the mood to work than she was. But it was Friday night and only a matter of time before the weekend madness began.

And then Erin wondered what she would do if Sebastian showed up again tonight when she wouldn't have but maybe a minute or two to talk. Not that talk had been a big part of their interaction so far...

"Okay, tell me how bizarre it is that we've been whining about having no man in our lives and we both get lucky within the same twenty-four hours."

Erin looked at Cali who was obviously way on her way to falling in love. While Erin was on her way to...what? Absolutely fabulous sex? Yes, that was it exactly. Exactly what she'd wanted when she'd hatched this Man To Do plan.

"I'm thrilled for you and Will. But I don't think what I'm doing with Sebastian qualifies as having a man in my life. More like having a man in my—" *body?* "—bed."

Cali lifted a brow. "That's what you wanted, though, isn't it?" When Erin hesitated, Cali quickly added, "I didn't have a tape recorder going but I'm quite sure I can quote you verbatim. You're tired, remember? Of double standards and men having all the fun and going to bed alone. Any of that ring a bell?"

What Erin was tired of was being reminded of things she'd said then that she wasn't sure she meant now. "Quite loudly, unfortunately."

"Unfortunately? So, you've changed your mind after one night?"

How could she explain this without going into graphic detail? "I just never expected one night to be..."

"To be what?" Cali scooted to the edge of her chair and leaned forward to prop her elbows on Erin's desk. "I'm all ears here."

It would help a lot if Erin knew what she'd expected

from those hours with Sebastian. And why the intensity of what they'd shared had blown her so thoroughly away. "Oh. Like I'm going to share details of my private life when you're over there holding out on me?"

"Hey, I'm an open book. What do you want to know?"

"Last I heard you were afraid sleeping with Will would screw up your friendship, and this was just last night, mind you. Since then, you've spent the better part of today writhing and naked? You mind telling me how you got from Thursday's point A to Friday's point B?"

"Actually we spent the better part of the day sleeping." Cali smiled a beatific smile. "It was the *best* part of the day we spent making love."

Making love.

Those words certainly didn't apply to the acts in which Erin and Sebastian had engaged, did they? Not only hadn't they made love, she wondered if they'd even made like. Or if they'd only been two improper strangers screwing themselves senseless. "What a difference a day makes, huh?"

"Or a night, anyway. I guess in my case it was the difference made by a very innocent kiss that turned things upside down."

"What innocent kiss?"

"It was yesterday, before we closed up last night and left. Will and I were talking and I'd been thinking about your Man To Do plan." Cali shrugged. "I couldn't help it. I leaned over and kissed him on the cheek."

"And then what?"

"Then I walked away and got back to work."

"You tease!"

"I suppose so, but I'd like to think of it more as flirting. It's not like I was going to say no if he asked."

"Which apparently he did."

"Several times. To my complete and utter delight."

"So, now what? Are you actually going to date a good friend? Or are you just going to sleep with him?"

"You mean like you and Sebastian?"

Erin tossed her pencil to the desk and shoved both hands back through her hair. "We really are pathetic, you know. Just yesterday you weren't sure about seducing Will. And now you're dealing with a possible relationship. All I wanted was sex. Which I got. But now I'm thinking I might want more."

"You want more? Or more with Sebastian? What's he like anyway? You haven't told me a thing about him. Except for that…gallows thing."

"Truthfully?" Erin shrugged. "There's not a lot to tell. We didn't do much talking."

"You just rolled around in bed."

"No. We never made it out of the shower." Erin looked at her hands, front and back. "I'm surprised I'm not still a prune. I also want to know what he pays for hot water."

"So, he has a thing for being clean. Or else he's a fish. What else?"

"He has about a thousand books."

"Books?"

"Books. He has those floor-to-ceiling shelves with a library ladder that rolls. Quite impressive actually."

"Hmm," Cali mumbled. "Literary and intellectual. Maybe even a librarian."

This time Erin pushed to her feet to pace. The more she thought about who Sebastian was and all the things she didn't know, the more frustrated she became. So much for her plan to keep emotions from the equation, to stay uninvolved. She wanted to know everything there was to know about him.

"Not a librarian, no. The intellectual I might give you. He's quiet. Doesn't say a lot though you can tell by his eyes that he never stops thinking. Whatever he does, he makes big bucks. His place is twice the size of mine and built-out like you wouldn't believe."

"Besides his love of books, then. What else did his place tell you?"

"He loves music, which I already knew. And he has a huge computer station. Totally state-of-the art equipment. Makes me wonder if he's a consultant of some type."

"What sort of consulting, do you think?" Cali was once again bright-eyed and curious. "What about the books? What do they tell you? Medical? Technical?"

Erin stopped pacing to think. "Actually, he's a virtual Barnes & Noble. Psychology. Paranormal occurrences. Homer and Shakespeare. Stephen King and Ryder Falco and John Grisham."

"So, the guy's well-read and well-monied. Interesting and intellectual. I guess that leaves you only one option?"

"Which is?"

"Stop thinking so much and get to work."

ERIN WAS STILL WEIGHING the pros and cons of black and white cookies when she glanced up to welcome the customer who'd just settled onto the stool at the bar and found herself looking into the eyes of Sebastian Gallo.

The most intense experience of her life had been

spent with this man and she didn't even know what to say.

And so she said, "Hello."

He remained silent, his steady focus launching a fleet of nerves into her veins. She held his gaze and her smile, though the longer he sat there unspeaking, the more wooden her expression became.

Finally, he reached out and took her hand in his, linking their fingers and running his thumb in a caress over the tip of hers. "How're you doing?"

Her heart thumped and thudded. "I'm doing good. You?"

"Still sorta squishy. Leaking. Dripping. But I'll dry out." His lips lifted into a slow sultry smile.

And she laughed, never wanting to let go of his hand but knowing she couldn't draw a draft telepathically. And one of her customers had just flagged her down.

She pulled her fingers from Sebastian's but made sure to keep the visual connection. She needed that much—she needed more—but that would do for now. "Do you want a beer? Glass of wine? It's on the house."

"I was thinking more along the lines of champagne."

A brow went up. She reached for a clean mug and made quick work of the customer's refill. "Celebrating?"

"I am, as a matter of fact," he said and leaned against the back of the stool, hooking his elbows over the railing, his knees spread wide and his feet braced on the lowest rung. "I thought you might join me."

Tonight he wore a wine-colored shirt in rich linen tucked into neat black wool pants. His glossy black hair picked up glints of the bar's lighting and his eyes were clear and attentive and bright.

Erin wanted to gobble him up. "I would. If I wasn't working." Two steps down the bar to deliver the beer. Two steps back. "Can I have a rain check?"

"You can have anything you want," he said and Erin's world went still.

"You might want to be careful what you're offering." Her voice hadn't even wavered once. Amazing when she was shaking all the way to the roots of her hair. "I'm liable to take you up on it."

"I intend for you to."

Whew, but he played the game well. This one was going to keep her on her toes. "You have a preference for your champagne?"

He kept his gaze on her as he considered. "Tell you what. Give me a beer. The champagne can wait until later."

Later? What did he have in mind for later? And was she included in his plans? "Great. I'll pick out a good one."

"Pick out the best. My treat."

She'd have to see what she could do. If expense was no issue, as he'd seemed to imply… Her interest was definitely piqued. "I'll keep that in mind. I'm sure I can come up with a suitable vintage. Unless you have a preference?"

One that tastes best sipped from bare skin, perhaps?

"Only that it's one you'll enjoy."

"That won't be a problem," she said because she knew that it wouldn't. She had a bit of a champagne fetish. She just wished she had a better handle on where to take this conversation because she found herself searching for wit instead of relaxing and enjoying his company.

She supposed that was what happened when two people skipped several of the natural steps to intimacy and went straight to bed. Might not hurt to read up on Desmond Morris....

"So, other than the fabulous atmosphere and the fabulous drinks and my fabulous company, what brings you here?" There. That ought to do to get things going. She opened the bottle of ale she'd chosen for him and poured.

"I'd say you covered all of it."

Exactly what she'd wanted to hear. Even knowing his response was nothing more than upping the tension strung high-wire taut, it was exactly what she'd wanted to hear. "You don't have the notebook you had with you last night."

"Last night I was working." He reached for the mug of ale, lifting it in a toast before drinking.

Working on what, she wanted to scream because this was like the worst sort of fingernail-pulling torture. Instead, she said, "And now it's Friday and you're done for the week."

He laughed, returning the mug to the bar. "Unfortunately, I'm never done."

He didn't elaborate but Erin seized the opening. "Tell me about it. This entrepreneurial business isn't all it's cracked up to be. Or, actually, it's more. More than I don't remember signing on for."

"You're obviously handling that more pretty damn well." He glanced around the bar, leaning forward and wrapping his hand around the mug. "You've always got a crowd in here."

"I do, yeah, but how would you know that?" He'd

been here exactly twice in the year she'd run the bar. Last night and now. If he'd been here before, when Paddington's belonged to Rory, well, she hadn't been here often enough then to have noticed, had she?

Grimacing, she added, ''You're not exactly a regular.''

''You have windows.''

''And you're a Peeping Tom?''

He grinned. ''Nope. Just a moth drawn to the flame.''

Oh, but she loved the way that sounded. The way tiny wings fluttered in her belly. ''How do you figure that?''

He shrugged one shoulder, twisted his mug back and forth on the cork coaster. ''I think best when in motion, when on my feet. And I can only pace the loft for so long.''

''So you walk the streets.''

He nodded, drank again. ''A regular creature of the night.''

Which brought to mind vampires, not moths. No, not moths at all, but hunger and darkness and needs satisfied only at night. She forced back a shiver as she pictured him striding with purpose in black boots and a long black duster, moving in the shadows, stalking his prey.

Stalking her.

The noise of the bar became nothing but a hum, a background drone swarming around her while Sebastian's gaze compelled her forward. She found herself leaning against the bar and into his personal space, space she wanted to crawl into as desperately as she wanted to pull him into her body.

Thank goodness Cali's timing was what it was because she came to the rescue, sliding to a stop beside Erin and banging her serving tray down on the bar. "I've had it with those two. I've totally had it. I swear, Erin. You're going to have to get another server to cover that table."

The Daring Duo. Erin had been waiting for Cali to boil over about the couple. "I'll send A.J. over to crash their party."

"Yeah, that would work." Cali shoved back her mop of hair and heaved a disgusted sigh. "Except he didn't show up for his shift."

"What?" Erin glanced up at the clock suspended above the center of the circular bar. "He should've been here an hour ago. Where have I been?"

"I have a feeling he won't be showing for any of his future shifts." Cali planted a hand on her hip. "I heard he was looking to get hired on at Courtland's."

The new jazz café opening the next block down was certain to be a competitive thorn in Erin's side. Great. Less than a month to get a replacement hired and trained. As a rule, not that much of a problem.

But with the party coming up… Erin sighed.

"Can I help?" Sebastian reached over and took hold of her hand, which obviously surprised Cali who responded with a questioning, "Uh, Erin?"

Erin glanced up, caught Cali's gaze cutting uncertainly to Sebastian and back. "Oh, I'm sorry. Cali, this is Sebastian Gallo, my upstairs, uh, neighbor. Sebastian, Cali Tippen. The only server here who gets to talk back to me because she's also my best friend."

"Hi, Cali." Sebastian tipped his head in greeting.

"Uh, Sebastian. Hey. It's nice to meet you." Totally distracted, she rubbed at the obvious headache building behind her forehead. "I'm sorry to bust in on you and

Erin like this but I've reached the end of my rope with two of our regular customers and having A.J. up and quit without notice means I'm stuck with The Daring Duo.''

"I hope he doesn't think he's going to be getting a good work reference,'' Erin grumbled, tossing Sebastian's empty bottle into the trash.

"I wouldn't even give him a character reference,'' Cali added.

But Sebastian turned the conversation an entirely different direction when he asked, "The Daring Duo?''

Cali rolled her eyes, shook her head, raised one stop-sign hand. "Don't even ask.''

Though Erin chuckled, she did feel Cali's pain. "It's simply a term of endearment for the couple sitting in the far booth behind you on the right. They're not as discreet as Cali—and as I—obviously wish they would be in their displays of affection.''

"Wrong, Erin,'' Cali interrupted. "Affection is a light brush of her lips to his cheek, or his arm wrapped around her shoulder. Maybe even their hands on the table with fingers entwined. I'll even give them hands under the table with fingers entwined.''

Cali's gaze brushed over Sebastian's hand still resting on Erin's before glancing back out into the room. "But we're talking about things going on under that table that might require the intervention of a good vice cop.''

At that, Sebastian laughed, releasing Erin's hand to lean back in his stool. Immediately she felt—and hated—the loss of warmth, not only from the contact of his hand but from his nearness. That personal space he'd abandoned when he'd shifted to sit back in his chair. Oh, she was going to have to watch out for this one.

"They're regulars then?" he asked of Cali.

"Regular pains-in-the-ass." She turned to Erin for backup, brow furrowing as she thought. "What? At least three or four nights a week, right?"

Erin went about wiping down the bar where the bottle of ale had been sitting. She nodded. "Three or four nights a week for six weeks or so. Same table. Same wine. Same R-rated behavior."

"And when it borders on X-rated, I'm the one stuck having to crash their party. I do have to admit that it's not as bad as a porno flick. But, still." Cali shuddered and, thinking further, shuddered again. "All that tongue-sucking business and the way she's always breathing hard. And then there's his belt that seems to always be unbuckled…it's just too close to voyeurism for this girl."

Sebastian seemed to consider the information then asked, "So, this is a fairly new relationship?"

"For us or for them?" Erin replied, answering his question with a question.

He smiled at that. "For you, of course. But I'm thinking for them as well."

"Why do you think that?" Cali asked.

"First blush of passion. Can't keep their hands off each other."

The idea made sense to Erin since keeping busy was the only way she'd managed so far to keep her hands off Sebastian. She glanced from him to Cali. "Newlyweds maybe?"

Cali shook her head. "I don't think so. Neither one of them is wearing a ring and, yes, I know that doesn't prove anything. But the idea of those two being married doesn't gel. Besides, if they were married, they'd be home in bed. Not in the bar.''

"Not necessarily." Both Erin and Cali turned when Sebastian spoke. He shrugged one shoulder, the burgundy-colored fabric molding to the muscles beneath. "Exhibitionism might have been part of their initial attraction. They enjoy the thrill of seeing what they can get away with. It's part of the high of arousal."

"So, saying they are married, and I'm not saying any such thing," Cali quickly added. "Then why no rings?"

"Part of their game. Wanting others to see." He leaned forward, his sharp green gaze snagging Erin's. "Wanting others to wonder."

"Just like we're doing now," she managed, though her voice resonated with no more sound than that of a whisper. And he wasn't even touching her. Only looking. Watching. Knowing she was remembering all the things they'd done.

"Exactly." He glanced up, taking in the placement of the track lighting. Then glanced back at Erin. "You might think about adjusting the lighting. Spotlight their table. See if that deters them."

"I'm afraid that might encourage them further." Oh, but this conversation would be so much easier if her gaze wasn't constantly drawn to his mouth as he talked. She was too well-versed in the things he could do with his lips and his mouth and her nerves buzzed with arousal's first stirrings.

"Yeah," Cali cut in. "Before we do anything to encourage them further, can we please reassign that table to another server?"

Erin laughed. "Yeah. I can do that."

"And hire someone to replace A.J.?" Cali begged.

Erin glanced at a pleading Cali. "Let me pull the applications I have on file. I'll put them on my desk. If you get a chance, maybe you can glance through them and see if you recognize any of the names. If you've worked with any of them or heard anything. Bad or good. Save me the grief down the road."

"Actually…" Cali tugged nervously on a lock of her hair. "I know someone who needs a job and would be perfect."

"Who?"

"Could we talk in the office for a minute. Nothing personal," Cali added for Sebastian's sake.

He waved off her apology. "Not a problem."

"Sure," Erin said. "I'll be right there. Let me check with the bunch at the end of the bar and get Robin to cover me. So, give me five minutes?"

"Yeah, that'll give me time to make a quick round through my tables. Hopefully I'll return without having my eyes singed out of their sockets." Cali picked up her tray and headed back onto the battlefield.

Erin chuckled, watched her best friend walk off, then turned her attention to Sebastian. "Can I get you anything else?"

He shook his head. "I'm set."

"Great." She wanted to ask if he'd be there when she got back, if he planned to wait for her, to hang out the rest of the night then strip her naked and take her with reckless abandon there on top of the bar.

Instead, she said, "I'll check back with you in a few."

He lifted his mug. "I'll be here."

His words made walking away only marginally easier to bear.

TEN MINUTES LATER, Erin walked into the office to find her best friend pacing the small space, serving tray gripped at her side and bouncing off her hip as she walked.

Erin wondered what was going on, why it was Cali who seemed nervous when it was Sebastian sitting at the bar and totally destroying Erin's concentration.

She pulled open the file drawer where she kept the employment applications and pulled out the folder that had grown admittedly slim. Most of the servers she'd originally hired had stayed on.

A few had left after opening, lured away by the newer establishments promising bigger crowds, megatips and a level of energy with which Paddington's had never tried to compete.

Erin had purposefully redesigned the wine and tobacco bar with intimacy in mind. Rory's pub had been a lot like that, a second home for his regular customers, a place where men were able to raise a pint and blow off steam at the end of a long working day.

The pint and steam concept hadn't changed. She'd just made a few adjustments to the ambience, keeping her fingers crossed that Rory wouldn't mind, yet still looking over her shoulder expecting his growling censure. A strange reaction since he'd never once growled.

Not even when she'd ditched any steady dedication to her studies and had, instead, used a chunk of the inheritance from her parents to finance a backpacking trek through Europe, where she'd played and feasted and made mad love from Rome to Lisbon with the first of her life's true loves.

True love. Ha!

She dropped the applications folder onto the desk and, when Cali jumped, crossed her arms over her chest and lifted an inquiring brow. "What's up with you?"

"Only about a million things. Most of them named Will Cooper." Cali stopped, turned, shook her head and waved off the question hanging on Erin's tongue. "But never mind Will. What is Sebastian doing here?"

Erin hadn't yet answered that question to her own satisfaction. She certainly didn't have an answer for Cali. "Besides making me extremely nervous? I have no idea. So forget Sebastian for the moment and tell me about Will. What's going on? You were all glowing when you talked about him earlier."

"I was not glowing. And he's not here yet, that's the problem. Which means he thinks sleeping with me was a mistake and I should've listened to my head instead of my heart." Cali snorted. "Or I guess it wasn't exactly my heart I was listening to, was it?"

Oh, poor baby. Erin braced both hands on her desk and leaned forward into Cali's space. "Yes, Dork. It was your heart. Otherwise you'd've been boinking Will a long time ago. You know that."

"I don't know anything."

"Well, I do. And I know he'll show up. I've watched you two together, Cali. Will's not the type to hit-and-run, if you know what I mean."

"Okay. You're right. I know he's not like that. I wouldn't want to be with him if he was." Cali buried her face in her hands. "Why does sex have to suck?"

"Because orgasms are really good that way?"

Cali chuckled, then laughed, then totally broke up into hysterical cackles and collapsed into Erin's chair to catch her breath. "That's not funny."

"Yes it is. Now, who do you know that's looking for a job and can I get a decent night's work out of him or her?'' Erin propped a hip on the corner of her desk. ''Or is the lure of all that jazz at Courtland's going to be hard to resist?''

Cali flipped through the short stack of applications. ''I doubt this would be long term, but I know it would get you out of the bind you're in for the party.''

''So, speak woman.''

''It's Will. The ad agency where he's been freelancing let him go.''

Erin wished all her business decisions were this easy. ''He can start tomorrow. Hell, he can start tonight the minute he gets here.''

''*If* he gets here, you mean.''

''Stop it already or I'm going to have to hurt you.'' Erin backed up toward the office entrance. ''Now, if he's out there when I open the door, you're going to owe me for putting up with all this ridiculous grief of yours.''

''If he's out there, I'll give you half of tonight's tip money.''

Erin knew what Cali made in tips. Half of the money would pay for more than a few black and white cookies. But the wager was hardly fair. She'd seen Will walk through the front door while on her way to the office.

Still…

''You're on, sister. But I'll stash the money in a safe place and add it to your honeymoon fund. I'm thinking Tahiti or Fiji. Sand and surf and sun and very little clothing. You could get by with a carry-on bag as long as it would hold all your condoms.''

''Oh, very funny,'' Cali said but her smile was firmly settled in place and the idea one Erin knew wouldn't be easily dislodged.

And wasn't that what best friends were for.

7

ERIN SET TWO FLUTES AND the ice bucket into which, thirty minutes ago, she'd placed a bottle of Perrier-Jouet on the table—the very table—occupied by The Daring Duo earlier tonight. Paddington's was closed, the room dark but for two brass lanterns that remained burning night and day, flanking the bar's heavy oak door and glinting off the stained glass inset.

She'd hurried the staff through the routine of close, keeping Robin and Laurie both longer than usual to help Cali set the bar room to rights. Will had helped as well, having been more than happy to accept Erin's offer of employment. He really was a good guy. Cali was a very lucky girl. Erin was thrilled the two had finally gotten together.

She herself had rushed through the register tapes and the cash drawers, the deposit of the evening's take and the accounting she had to make each night of stock to be reordered and the labor percentage costs versus the total receipts. The analysis of those numbers, however, would have to wait until tomorrow.

Whether or not she rushed or lingered now, she'd have to go over the books again in the morning. Because, no matter how much time she took tonight, her mind was elsewhere and even Rory looking over her shoulder couldn't guilt her into forgetting about the man waiting for her in the bar.

Forget about Sebastian Gallo. As if.

Tonight, in fact, she'd gone so far as to bring to work a change of clothes, a washcloth and a bottle of her favorite chamomile shower gel. Once she'd finished with the books, she'd taken full advantage of the private office bathroom to pull off her monogrammed polo and gabardine pants. She'd washed away the sweat of the last few hours then changed into the sexy lace bra she wished she'd been wearing yesterday.

Donning her long black skirt and soft cashmere sweater, she did what she could to check herself out using the warped dressing room mirror hanging on the back of the door. After twisting and turning in the restrictive space, she decided that, as long as she didn't really look as distorted as her funhouse reflection, the emerald green was a very good choice judging by the sparkle in her eyes.

So, by the time she locked up after the others, made with the quick sponge bath and retrieved the champagne, she was frantic Sebastian would've given up on her and left.

Finding him should've set her mind at ease.

What it did was make her wet.

She slid into the small circular booth, sitting beside him though she left several inches of space between their bodies. She wanted to share the champagne and the celebration. She wanted to be far enough from him to be able to look into his eyes. She wanted the distance because she wanted the temptation of closing it.

Never before had she known a sweeter taboo than Sebastian Gallo. A taboo because he should've been off-limits and out of her reach, physically, emotionally, definitely sexually. Yet a taboo she couldn't resist because he fit so perfectly into her plans. Yes. That was the reason. He was her Man To Do. That was the source of this incredible fascination. It was all about the forbidden, the unexpected, the thrill of the unknown.

Or so she repeatedly told herself.

"So, this is The Daring Duo's table?" He opened the champagne, smoothly managing the pop of the cork, equally smoothly filling both flutes.

Tiny bubbles danced in the cold, tempting Erin to drink and savor the crisp tingle. "The very one. But it should be safe. Will wiped down all the benches, Laurie mopped, and Robin replaced the tablecloth."

The dark indigo and wine fabric brushed Erin's knees when she crossed her legs, legs left bare beneath the long skirt. As bare as her bottom *sans* panties or thong. She wanted to be ready for whatever Sebastian had in mind and had dressed appropriately—or undressed, as it were.

Besides, she had her own mind wrapped around a few fantasies where clothing would only be in the way. "Do you really think they're married? Putting on a show for our benefit?"

Sebastian sipped, paused, sipped again then downed nearly half the contents of his flute. He didn't answer Erin's question directly, but poured himself another drink, turning on one hip to better face her.

"Their show isn't for our benefit, Erin." He ran his finger around the flute's fragile rim. Around and around, hypnotically. "It's for their own. It's what turns them on, knowing people are watching. It gets him hard. It makes her wet. They use the knowledge of being watched the same way you might use a vibrator." He looked up then, his gaze heated and compelling. "Or the same way I might use a hot shower."

Erin didn't even know what to say. She wasn't sure she could breathe. She remembered too well his hot shower and the memory of the way she'd watched, the way he'd taken himself in his hand and stroked to completion, the way she'd wanted to wrap her mouth around the plum-ripe and plump head and enjoy his taste as much as give him pleasure.

But she wasn't going to talk about her vibrator because more often than not her fantasies were lived with only her hands. And, lately, she'd imagined her hands to be his. But she did want to understand about his shower. The decadence of space and design, the potential for hedonistic indulgence, had not been lost on her. Had, in fact, been demonstrated quite clearly.

So…why?

"Tell me about your hot showers. About that space. The benches. The showerheads. That's not…" She fluttered one hand, reaching for her flute. "That's not the bathroom of a man who only showers to wash his body. It intrigues me." She lifted the flute to her lips and, before she sipped she added, "You intrigue me."

She watched as emotion flickered through his eyes, truth battling fiction, real involvement fighting the tempting attraction of a casual affair.

And she knew whatever he told her, if he told her anything at all, that she would never know with any certainty if he'd chosen to let honesty win the war with the fantasy of a provocatively spun yarn.

Or if he'd only told her what he wanted her to believe in order to keep them wrapped up in this sensual spell.

He inched his way closer, his thigh and hip brushing hers. He draped an arm on the curve of the seat back and toyed with strands of her hair. His gaze was wickedly sharp as it snagged hers and held. "I shower to think."

Erin's pulse jumped at the contact. If he moved any closer, if his touch grew more intimate... She might as well give up now on any sort of coherent thought. "You told me you walked to think."

"I do both."

"Depending on what you need to think about?" she asked and sipped at her champagne.

He nodded, fingering the fragile stem of his own half-filled flute. "Depending on what I need to work out in my mind. Walking is about fresh thinking. Getting the blood to flow to my brain."

"And the hot showers? That amazing piece of real estate you call a bathroom?" She *would* get to the bottom of this if it killed her. Or if it took her all night— even though she was quite certain all that heat and water was about blood flowing to other parts of his body.

He took the flute from her hand and set it on the table. "The showers should be obvious. The steam straightens out the wrinkles the walking puts in my brain."

That caught her off guard and she chuckled, then reached for her flute again but he took hold of her hand and stopped her. She stared at his much larger hand covering hers that was so much smaller. "I never realized certain thinking was done better under certain conditions."

"But you do it all the same." He laced their fingers together, studied her short, practical nails.

"No. I don't have that luxury." Though even as she refuted his claim she realized she thought more about her issues with Paddington's while at the bar, thought more about the missing needs of her personal life while at home.

''It's not a luxury. It's what I do.'' He reached for her other hand, holding both of hers in both of his, and she shifted on the bench to better face him. ''You do it more than you realize. I'm just more conscious of where I need to be, what I need to be doing in order to get my head on straight.''

Her head would never be on straight. Not when he was making love to her hands, massaging her fingers and the base of her thumbs, her palms, her knuckles, the pads at the tips of her fingers. His touch seduced her and made concentrating on this strange conversation more than difficult.

Nearer to impossible. As was any cognizant reply. ''You think too much about thinking.''

''Thinking's what I do.''

That was the second time he'd said that and she knew the remark was worth pursuing. But, at the moment, she wasn't able to pursue anything at all. She was relaxed and hypnotized by what he was doing to her hands.

Maybe he was a street magician, a magic man like David Blaine, the legal pad filled with notes on the tricks of the trade, all that thinking he did part of the process of working out the subtleties of deception.

It all made sense, she supposed, except she wasn't supposed to be wondering about who he was and what he did because she was only here for his body, not his mind. Or so she continually worked to convince herself wondering if she'd ever succeed.

So when he took her hands he was holding, cupped her palms and covered her breasts with their joined hands, she forgot all about his shower and his thinking because the lantern light had turned his eyes to a compelling contrast of light green and dark desire from which she couldn't pull her gaze.

He pressed his forefingers and thumbs to her forefingers and thumbs and worked her hands over her nipples. She gasped, unable to hold back her response because it was the response of her fantasy. This was her fantasy. Her hands that were his hands arousing her darkest desire.

"When I was a boy," he began, his hands leaving hers and moving to the tiny pearl buttons of her sweater, "I lived on the streets. I never knew anything about my father. All I remember of my mother could be called selective. Only the things I want to recall."

"Is this true?" she asked, her hands growing still on her breasts as her focus switched from his touch on her body to the touch of his words on her mind.

"Don't ask questions. Just listen."

He continued to release her buttons, each tiny seed pearl slipping easily through the grosgrain ribbon facing the cashmere placket. One button, then another, air kissing her skin as the two sides began to part.

Yet, she remained silent, wanting to hear and to feel. Her hands fell to her lap as she concentrated her focus on his voice and his hands.

"I had a toy truck. One wheel was missing, but I didn't care. I sort of liked that it had to fight against the odds, bumping along the way it did." He reached the bottom of the unending row of buttons, his knuckles brushing the fabric of her skirt where it covered her belly.

"I rolled it across every inch of the concrete floor in the building where I lived. A building with no glass in the windows. Cardboard didn't do much against the wind, but that's all that was left with the plywood having been burned for heat. The ashes made for a great construction site.''

Erin listened to his story, wishing he was doing no more than entertaining her, lulling her with the magic of his words, seducing her with the magic of his hands. But she knew that wasn't the case, that he was doing much more than that. That what he was telling her wasn't any sort of tale at all, but the truth she'd been hoping to find.

His timing totally sucked, she grumbled, because how was she supposed to concentrate on what he was saying when he had opened the front of her sweater and was, even now, pushing it back off her shoulders?

His gaze devoured the ecru lace that made up the cups of her bra, lace through which her nipples strained and pouted. He reached for her champagne flute and sipped, then rubbed the wet rim beneath her nipple, over and around before he poured champagne over her breast and leaned his head down to drink.

The sensation caught her struggling to breathe. The air on the damp lace was cool, his mouth was hot, his tongue swirling and circling, his lips sucking the peak into an unbearable tightness rivaling that in her chest, making it hard for her to catch her breath.

Harder still for her trembling heart to beat.

When he finally lifted his head, Erin wondered, what next? What now? How would she ever get enough of what he did to her body? And how long was she going to manage to keep her emotions uninvolved when he told her stories of little boys and their trucks?

''I don't know how old I was when I was finally picked up. My mother had long been gone. When I wanted to try and get a handle on the timing of things,

I remembered the birthday cupcake she must have begged from a bakery. I used that and counted forward. She told me we were celebrating the first day of spring and making it through the last five years. So, I must've been eleven—or close to it—when the authorities managed to get their hands on me.''

All the while he'd been speaking, he'd worked the straps of her bra off her shoulders, trapping her in sleeves of cashmere and the bra's ecru lace. Yet it was the bondage of his gaze that kept her still.

He studied her quandary then reached around to free her arms and release the clasp holding her bra in place. The sweater dropped to the seat behind her. The bra fell to her lap, baring her full breasts that ached for his attention.

''Come here,'' he ordered and pulled her onto his lap.

The edge of the table gouged into her back but she hardly noticed. She was too aware of his erection solidly pressed between her thighs and his hands and mouth that were everywhere at once. Kneading flesh so incredibly sensitive and dying for his touch.

She held on to his shoulders because it was all she could do, and tossed her head back, feeling like the wanton she knew she had to look. She spread her legs wider, her skirt bunching around her thighs as she ground against him, wanting him there where she was so incredibly wet and ready and open.

He blew a long breath onto her skin between her breasts where his face was buried. And then he moved a hand between his own legs and stroked his erection before reaching deeper and pressing hard to halt what he could of the surging sensation.

He shuddered, and his hand found its way up between *her* legs, to the very spot where she was naked and waiting. His second breath heated her skin and a string of raw curses followed. In the next moment she found herself filled by the thick length of two fingers.

She arched toward his lower body but all he did was widen the V of his spread legs, forcing her thighs farther open there where she sat on his lap. His thumb circled her clit; his tongue circled her nipple.

She braced her hands on his shoulders and rode his thrusting fingers hard, wanting more, wanting to wait, wanting him now even while wanting to draw out the anticipation until both of them were ready to burst.

And just when she was ready to come, he pulled his hand away, moved his mouth away and sat back, his chest heaving beneath raw and ragged breaths.

"Why did you stop?" she panted.

"I'm not ready for you to come."

To hell with what he was ready for. She was ready enough to take matters into her own hands, to get herself off to the fantasy she'd grown practiced to using, and groaned when he stopped the downward reach of her fingers.

"Not yet," he bit off.

"You're making me crazy."

"I want you wetter."

Wetter? Moisture seeped from her sex to run into the crevice of her thigh. She smelled her own musk and saw his nostrils flare. She doubted it was possible to be any wetter. She wasn't sure she'd ever been this wet.

"I swear, Sebastian. You're out of your mind. You don't think this is wet enough?"

"Trust me," he said moving his hands to her waist and boosting her to sit onto the edge of the table. She pushed herself upward with the heels of her palms. Then he slid his hands up her calves to her knees beneath her skirt. "Lean back."

She hesitated, but did as he asked, knowing she was putting herself in an incredibly vulnerable position, yet unable to stop the thrilling, edgy flutter of nerves.

Sebastian pulled his hands from under her skirt and settled his palms on her thighs, inching the soft black fabric upward until her skirt rode high. The thought that she was so close to being spread across the table, a feast for his consumption, ripe fruit for his hedonistic indulgence…

She tossed back her head, stopped short of releasing the bubbling laughter, uncertain whether what she was feeling was nervousness, wickedness or total disbelief that she was actually so incredibly bold.

He shimmied her skirt up farther until his thumbs found the skin of her inner thighs. He rubbed there, small circles, inching closer to the crease where leg met hip. If nothing else, he'd certainly mastered a very effective method of torture. She was panting, in pain, and ready to scream.

He leaned forward, kissed her thigh, blew a stream of breath against her skin, ran his tongue along the patch he'd just heated. He repeated the action on the opposite side, only this time he moved closer to her sex. He shifted forward, returned to the leg where he'd started, repeated the process and proved her earlier assumption totally wrong.

She was wetter, more ready, more aroused than she'd been minutes before when he'd made love to her with his fingers. She could not believe the intensity of her own incredible response. The way flames licked through her body's center. The way her skin sizzled from the inside out.

This time, when he moved closer, he pushed her skirt up over her hips to her belly, completely exposing her nakedness, and leaned in to blow a stream of hot breath from her clitoris down between her legs, blowing directly into the mouth of her sex and then blowing lower still.

The waiting, the Tantric sense of anticipation and denial would've been fun if she didn't ache quite so badly, didn't yearn quite so wildly to find her completion. She didn't think she'd ever been so desperate to come. And Sebastian's obsession with arousing her further, the concentrated sensation of his hands and his mouth...five minutes more and she'd be out of her mind.

And then he returned to his tale. "I spent six years living off the State. We had a locker room set up where we showered. A dorm's worth of teenage boys all at one time, looking over our shoulders, watching our backs, hoping to make it through those quick fifteen minutes without the need for stitches and our virginity intact."

Erin pulled in a sharp breath. His shocking words hit her at the same time he gently pressed the knuckle of his thumb into the crevice between her legs and dragged it down. She wanted to think about what he was saying, tried to think about what he was saying, but couldn't get beyond what he was doing and doing so incredibly, amazingly well.

"I showered like that four times a week for six or seven years. I did okay. I made it out. And I swore whenever I finally got on my feet and could afford a place of my own, I would never again worry about hot water or how long I spent taking a bath.''

All the while he'd been talking, he'd been watching the play of his fingers in and around her sex. Erin could easily have gotten off twice now. But she'd gritted her teeth and listened to his story. Still braced back on her elbows, she'd tucked her chin to her chest and kept her gaze trained on Sebastian's face.

Never once had he hesitated in the telling of his story and never once had he looked up to see if she was listening or if she'd dissolved into a mass of writhing sexuality which so aptly described the sensations in her belly and below. Twisting, twining, kinky knots and ropes of enflamed nerves.

When at last he sat back, she knew he was ready. Or so she thought until he picked up the champagne bottle and used it to stroke along both her inner thighs. He moved the bottle higher, rubbing the mouth over the lips of her sex and between, circling her clit, slipping the cool glass along her folds, down one side, up the other, teasing her unmercifully before finally lifting the bottle to drink.

Yet, even as he swallowed, even as Erin waited breathlessly for him to return the bottle to the table, pull a condom from his pocket and set himself free, he drizzled champagne there above her strip of trimmed hair and leaned forward, drinking both the wine and her moisture from between the folds of her sex.

Erin couldn't take it any longer. She cried out, her body rigid beneath the shattering sensations of orgasm, the rush of pleasure sending her arching upward toward his mouth. Her flesh tingled and burned and throbbed, and still she came because this wasn't enough. She needed to have him inside her.

She pushed up from her elbows, pushed Sebastian away and against the back of the booth. She reached for the waistband of his pants. He reached into his pocket. She longed to stroke him, to watch his eyes glaze, to draw forth that first bead of moisture telling her he was ready to come.

But she doubted they'd ever be able to take their time coming together because of this combustible fire between them. He tore into the condom packet and rolled the sheath the length of his erection. Erin didn't even ask. She slid off the table and into his lap, her hand between their bodies to guide him to her center.

He filled her, and it was like finding a part of herself that had been missing. The fit was snug and perfect. She gripped him with muscles still sore from last night. With her hands braced on his shoulders, his hands on her waist, she rode him hard. Her breasts swayed and he pressed his forehead against her chest, panting hot ragged breaths there in the valley between.

Her thigh muscles burned from exertion. Her pulse raced, the blood in her veins fairly sang. She was raw from the friction of his late evening beard, raw from the flat of his tongue, raw from the thick scraping slide of his cock and she didn't even care. This was what she'd wanted. This aching, bursting, joyous connection of bodies in need.

Sebastian spread his legs wider, slumped down onto his spine and drove himself upward, his head pressed back into the padded booth, the tendons in his neck drawn taut. She wanted to ease his torture, his agony, but the strain on his gorgeous face only incited her further.

She came again, his thrusts wild and urgent, spurring her over the edge. Guttural groans of release ripped from his throat as he joined her. She collapsed against his chest, tremors shuddering through her. She missed the feel of his bare skin against hers. But urgency hadn't given him time to undress beyond exposing his sharply cut abs when he'd shoved his pants down his hips.

His heart thudded with hers in a matching beat. Her heated breath condensed on his neck where she'd rested her head and she inhaled the scent of his skin the way she inhaled the aroma of coffee in the morning. A necessity to her very existence. She doubted she could ever get enough of breathing him in.

Or a more fulfilling sense of her world being right as she rested against him, his arms around her back holding her close, his body buried in hers still pulsing in response to her last lingering quakes.

This was the high she'd been physically craving, this sated sense of exhaustion on the heels of mind-blowing sex. She didn't think she'd ever known such satisfaction of body.

It was the satisfaction of soul that she wasn't sure she could bear.

CALI CROSSED HER LEGS AND scooted closer to the coffee table. She sat on the floor in front of Will's futon, digging into the huge banana split they shared. Will sat similarly on the other side. Their knees bumped beneath the low table.

They both wore white T-shirts, gray sweatpants and thick athletic socks, compliments of Will's wardrobe. The ice cream was a middle of the night feast celebrating his new job at Paddington's and the last two hours they'd spent in bed.

Cali wasn't sure she'd ever spent a more perfect Friday night in her life.

He'd been such a great sport and so much fun to work with while they'd helped Erin close up for the night. When he'd suggested they eat a late dinner and had even volunteered to cook, she'd jumped at the chance. This girl wasn't no fool. By the time they reached his apartment, of course, neither one of them was in the mood for food.

She figured the ice cream would sate the hunger in her empty tummy until they got around to something more substantial after sleeping off the sugar and the sex. Ah, yes. And what sex it was. Her body sang with satisfaction, thanking her for the dual indulgence. So what if she got up off the floor having gained five pounds?

Will didn't seem to care that she was curvy rather than willowy and gaunt. Seemed, in fact, to totally enjoy the fact that she didn't gouge him with fashionably protruding hipbones. A good thing, too, because she really liked the way his body felt cradled on top of hers. And she loved that he wanted to be there…though maybe *love* wasn't the best word to use.

Sighing, she turned her spoon over onto her tongue and licked it clean of caramel and chocolate sauce then used the bowled end as a pointer. "You know I'm going to have to totally cram tomorrow to catch up before Monday's class."

"You mean you're going to totally have to cram *today*." Will scooped up a huge bite of mostly whipped cream and maraschino cherry bits.

Cali groaned. "It is today, isn't it? Saturday already. How come when I'm with you I totally lose track of time?"

Will pulled his spoon from his mouth, slowly shoveled it into the mountain of Blue Bell Homemade vanilla ice cream, Hershey's chocolate syrup and about a dozen other toppings from M&M's to chopped pecans.

He left the spoon standing upright, braced his elbows on the table and leaned forward into Cali's space. His eyes twinkled like snifters of brandy in firelight. "Do you really want me to answer that?"

She considered for only half a minute or so whether she'd consumed enough energy-laden carbs to have another go in the bedroom, or if the sugar would knock her out before she could get his clothes off, not to mention her own.

Then she decided she'd been far too easy every time they'd been naked and this time, if there was going to be a this time here in the middle of their ice cream feast, she was going to make Will work a little bit harder.

Even with the extra five pounds added onto her original extra fifteen, she was worth the effort. She really wasn't as easy as the last two days made her out to be. And she didn't want him to think she'd desperately been waiting around for him to take an interest and notice her. Or to find out he'd taken pity on her after seeing her heart on her sleeve—an accusation Erin leveled way too often.

Cali pulled up the boot straps of her self-esteem, aware that she'd picked a strange time to get prickly over her sexuality and desire for Will. Especially coming on the tail end of her reminiscing. "No, I don't need to hear your man-sex answer. I can answer perfectly well for myself."

Chuckling under his breath, Will shook his head and

retrieved his spoon and a mouthful of banana. "This I gotta hear."

Deep breath, Cali. Take a deep breath. This was not the time to get all teary-eyed and emotional which, for an inexplicably hormonal reason, she felt ready to do. That meant she needed to turn the conversation in a new direction. And she knew exactly where to go. "The time we're together passes quickly because all you want to do is argue down every one of my ideas for Jason's role in the screenplay."

Will's easy smile vanished, replaced by stoicism and that stubborn male need to always be right. "That's bull, Cali. I'm not arguing down anything. I know as well as you do that without Jason we don't have a screenplay. It's his story."

At least they agreed on that one unarguable point. Now to get Will to understand how and where the rest of his story logic didn't hold water. "Exactly. Which is why our obsession with the external action is diluting the focus."

"This isn't some trendy art house idea." He attacked the ice cream with a vengeance, jabbing his spoon repeatedly into the same crevice. "Didn't we agree on that early on? That we're writing for the big screen? Which means, duh, we need action?"

Cali really hated to pull out the big guns but it was the discussion they'd had the first day of their screenwriting class that had gotten them here in the first place.

Each class member had been asked by the professor to name the one screenwriter or screenplay that most impacted his or her decision to study the craft. The discussion that followed had sealed the fate she now shared with Will.

And so she prodded him with a gentle reminder. "Christopher McQuarrie. *The Usual Suspects*. Nineteen-ninety-five Academy Award for Best Writing of a Screenplay Written Directly for the Screen."

Will shook his head, glanced up at her from beneath his long lashes, unable to hold back a twist of a smile. "The sucker was brilliant. Totally brilliant."

Yes! Now they were getting somewhere. "The movie or the writer?"

"Both. Same thing. And you know that's what I want to do," he said, abandoning the spoon he'd been stabbing hard down into the bowl.

"Well it's not going to happen if you don't do for our Jason Coker what Christopher McQuarrie did with Keyser Soze."

Will's smile froze, then faded. "And you don't think that's what I'm doing."

"I *know* that's not what you're doing," she said quickly before she stopped to think about Will's feelings, or anything but the honesty of her answer.

A look of defeat clouded his expression. "So, what do I do? Start at the beginning? Analyze this beast one element at a time and see what I'm missing?"

Cali spoke hurriedly again, same reason, same possible regrets. Hoping he didn't come totally unglued when he heard her off-the-wall proposal, one that had started as a niggling itch last night. "You know, I have an idea. I really can't say why I think this makes sense, just that it does."

"Well, what? Speak up, woman."

She placed her hands palms down against the table on either side of the huge crystal bowl, wishing she had a better surface into which she could wrap her fingers and hold on. "This is totally out of left field, I know, but why don't we give a rundown of our idea to Sebastian and see what he has to say."

Will blinked, frowned, frowned harder. "Sebastian? Gallo? Why do you think he'd have any valuable input?"

"Something." She shrugged, toying with her spoon, pulling it slowly through the ice cream mountain in an effort to dig a deep enough trench to use for her grave. She had a feeling she was going to need it. "I'm not sure. I don't know."

"Well, yeah, then. I can see how that would make sense," Will huffed, pushing up from his crossed feet to stand. He began to pace in short jagged turns.

Cali pulled her knees to her chest, wrapped her arms around them in a tight hug and leaned back against the futon. "Before you got to Paddington's tonight? Erin and I were telling Sebastian about The Daring Duo. You know, the couple in *that* booth?"

"Yeah." Will snorted, shoving an agitated hand back over his hair. "The ones you and Erin are always talking about."

Cali frowned at that. "Actually, they're not the only ones we talk about and, no, it's not a stellar quality we share. More like a big fat personality flaw. But there are just some people who tend to rev up the ol' curiosity, ya know? And so we make up stories."

"I see," he said with a roll of his eyes to go with the rest of his high-handedness.

Uh-uh. She wasn't going to put up with this crap. Not from him. Not ever from him. "Oh, get over yourself already, Will. I've heard what you've said about more than a few of our fellow students, not to mention a professor or two."

"Yeah, yeah, whatever." He remained frowning but

it was almost an expression of being taken aback. And his tone had softened. "So, what's this deal about Sebastian. What do you know about him anyway?"

Deep breath in. Deep breath out. Okay, she'd yelled and he hadn't run off—or anything worse. This was a good thing. "Not much, really. Erin's only been seeing him a few days, though he's lived in her building since she moved in."

"Hmm. I wondered what the connection was," he said and finally stopped pacing.

"She didn't pick him up in the bar or off the street if that's what you're asking." Though, Cali decided, choosing Sebastian as a Man To Do made it nothing but a matter of semantics. "It just wasn't the right time for them to get together. Not until recently."

She held her breath, waiting for Will to comment on the coincidence that the two of them had finally gotten together at the very same time. The very same day, in fact, though no way was she going to tell him about the Man To Do article, or how Erin's decision to go after Sebastian had impacted Cali's determination to explore her chemistry with Will.

But he didn't say anything so she continued to fill the silence. "I'm not sure I know what else to say. He picked right up where we stalled out, making up a story about who they might be and how they got together. It was so cool."

Hands at his hips, Will stood on the other side of the table and stared down. "And because of that you want him to advise us on our idea? Don't you think that's stretching it a bit, Cali?"

Her idea had merit; she knew it did. She was not going to let his ego knock it down. "You know, Will, just because he's not in our class or an expert doesn't mean he wouldn't have good instincts about the story.''

''*I* have good instincts about the story. And *I'm* your study and project partner. Not Sebastian Gallo.''

Argh! Save her from hardheaded men. This one in particular. ''I know who you are, Will. And I know Sebastian has nothing to do with our project. It's just that we've been so wrapped up in what we're doing I'm afraid tunnel vision is setting in. And I don't see how a fresh pair of eyes could hurt anything. It's not taking away from any of the work you've done, or we've done, it's just…''

''It's just that forest for the trees thing, isn't it?'' he asked, circling around to drop onto the futon. He lay back, one knee up, a forearm thrown over his forehead even while he stared wide-eyed at the ceiling.

Cali swiveled around where she sat on the braided rug covering the hardwood floor. She leaned an elbow on the futon mattress and propped her head in her hand. He looked so exhausted, and it had to be about more than the screenplay. He had just lost his job, after all.

She had no idea if he was worried about money but she suspected the blow had hit him harder than he intended to let her know, even if the strike was more to his ego than his wallet. She wished she could kiss it and make it all better. Instead she did the next best thing, resting her hand on his chest and rubbing tiny circles with her fingertips.

He moved his hand to cover hers and sighed. ''You're probably right. We've been working on this without a break for two months and I'm getting ragged.'' He turned his head and looked, really looked, into her eyes. ''How are you?''

Now that you're here? I don't think I've ever been

so good. She smiled. "Exhaustion is my life. But I'll live."

He toyed with one of her curls. "I didn't thank you for putting in a good word with Erin."

Cali beamed. "I hardly put in a word at all. She jumped on you like…well, like I've been jumping on you the last couple of days." *Like I could jump on you now,* she thought, even though all she wanted to do was jump into his arms and wrap him up tight.

"And what's stopping you now?" he asked, his tender smile negating the lecherous waggle of both brows.

And that was all it took. She climbed up next to him and snuggled into his body. When he wrapped himself around her and pulled her close, breathing deeply as he drifted off to sleep, she knew she was exactly where she was meant to be.

8

Chapter 5

She'd found him.

He hadn't been clever enough or quick enough; he hadn't even been aware enough of where he was to duck. He had, in fact, seen her coming and all he'd done was sit behind the wheel of his car and watch as she'd walked his way.

The night had been pitch-black. The hour as late as it got. He'd been parked down the block from the building he'd seen her enter. Not the building his partner still covered from the other side. Not the building where they'd find the dealer scum they'd been after for weeks.

Raleigh couldn't believe it but he was so incredibly fucked right now. His career, his life, hell, even his mind. And it was too late to see if he couldn't get this right the second time around.

There wasn't going to be a second time.

This was it.

She walked toward him.

What the hell had he been thinking, blowing off the job he was paid to do? And all because of a distraction that he should have seen coming. That

he was trained to see coming. That was coming
right toward him.

Now it was too late.

She was here and he was done for. Fried up
like battered frog legs to taste just like chicken.
Yum, yum…

Crap. Pure and total crap.

Sebastian shoved away from his desk and headed for
his bedroom window. His chair rolled backward across
the room to bounce off his highboy dresser, sending
Redrum skittering and scratching across the hardwood
floor.

What in the hell was wrong with him? He couldn't
even string together a sentence that didn't sound
like…pulp. Garbage. Bird-cage liner. Camp-fire fuel.

Raleigh wasn't the only one with a career in the
toilet. Sebastian might as well pay back his advance
and stake out a prime street corner, a successful pan-
handler's first plan of action. One he knew well.

It was early Saturday morning, not yet dawn. The
city was silent without the workday noise to which he
usually climbed into bed. The air was cool, crisp and
clean but for the bite of diesel from the trucks down
the street in the *Houston Chronicle* loading dock. He
stared at the police cruiser rolling by seven stories below.

What the hell had he been thinking, telling Erin the
things he had about his life in lock-up. He could only
hope she hadn't believed a word he'd said, that she'd
blown it all off as bunk he'd made up for her entertainment. A safety net of sorts so she could pretend she
hadn't let a virtual stranger go down on her in the middle of the bar.

He sure as hell didn't want her coming to the ridiculous conclusion that he'd purposely pointed out the one and only chink in his armor, enabling her in finding a way in. He didn't want her to find a way in. No matter that, in too many ways, she was already there, working to dismantle his tightly held independence. Working to convince him that he didn't have the grasp he claimed on his gentler emotions.

He figured she'd feel better about herself if he fed her a story to chew on. He sure didn't want her feeling bad about any of what they'd done. He wanted her to feel good. Damn good. As good as he was feeling. And that was saying a lot because he was supposed to be an expert at turning a cold shoulder and walking away. From involvement. From caring. From concern for another's emotions as well as from his own.

Those were the tenets that had gotten him through his teenage years and had carried him into adulthood. Why would he be so asinine as to open himself up, to invite a woman into his private life after all this time? Yet, in ways and levels he couldn't put into words, he had. And she'd accepted, both the invitation and the man he was.

He'd deny it all—the invitation, the emotional lapse—if she asked. He'd go on to tell her he'd been exercising his right to dramatic license. The story definitely fell into the realm of far-fetched. *That* much he figured she'd buy.

Shifting a hip onto the window, he swung his legs through to stand on the tiny fire escape ledge. The sky was awash in the first strokes of indigo and soon, very soon he'd need to turn in. The hour he now went to bed was the same hour he'd been rousted out for longer than he cared to remember.

Before spilling his guts to Erin, he'd never told another person about those years. Hell, the only person he'd even talked to at any length during that nonexistent time in his life had been Richie Kira. Richie, who'd been the closest thing Sebastian had ever had to a friend.

The sixty-year-old inmate had worked in the detention center's library, helping the kids confined to the facility with research and reading and any other information their instructor assigned them to find. Richie had sensed Sebastian's innate curiosity, a young boy's thirst for knowledge dying to be quenched.

The older man had introduced him to the vastly amazing worlds found on the shelves, between the pages of the books Richie had tended like a gardener would tend a prizewinning rose bed. Or like a farmer would tend the fields of corn and wheat that provided his livelihood. The comparison wasn't that far off the mark.

Books were Richie's connection with a life outside prison he hadn't seen in over forty years. But he read, and he remembered, and he told it all to Sebastian. Stories of war and women. Of football games and fights with neighborhood gangs. Of fast cars and loud music and how to kiss a girl so she never forgot your name.

He'd been the father Sebastian had never had, the mentor he'd needed, one who had advised him on the ways of the world without couching his words from a parent's perspective. He hadn't couched his words at all, but had instead let fly with advice straight off the street.

Advice from the prison yard, too.

Sebastian had gotten real good at watching his back

and cutting his losses. He'd just never expected to have to watch his front.

Richie might've taught lessons in female anatomy and birth control but never in dealing with the female mind. Or explained the way a woman's eyes had of sparkling like a beckoning finger right before landing a gut-slamming punch.

Three hours ago Sebastian had walked Erin to her front door. She'd wanted him to come in. He'd wanted to do just that, to walk into her loft and drag her off to bed. And so he'd told her goodbye there in the hallway and walked to the elevator, feeling both the heat and the uncertainty of her gaze on his back all the way.

He'd come home and poured his energy into his work in progress, well aware of his looming deadline but still unable to concentrate long enough to put more than a few words down on the page. Words that stank like week-old shit.

No matter how hard he tried to concentrate on Raleigh Slater, to get into the character's head, to slip into his skin and feel the terror gnawing at the detective's insides, Sebastian found his muse flirting with that *other* idea.

The one he'd been putting off until the right time. A story that didn't belong to Raleigh at all. That obviously didn't belong to Sebastian either since his muse had taken total control. The idea frightened him half to death, as did the implicit demand that he'd have to devote all his time and attention to the social order of his fictional world.

He wouldn't have time for Erin. And that caused a strange sort of jolt to the rhythm of his heart.

He stepped back into his bedroom, his foot skating over Redrum's back as the cat skulked toward the bed.

Sebastian nearly broke an ankle, tripping across the floor, and the damn cat did nothing but jump into the center of his bed. Typical female. Sneaking up to blind-side him.

Sebastian grabbed his chair and hauled it back to his desk, rolling up to his keyboard. The distraction of Erin Thatcher was beginning to make more sense. He wasn't focused. He wasn't concentrating. He was letting his muse have her way, giving in to her temptation, embracing the flow of creative juices and the energizing high.

That left enough of a gap in his absorption with his work for disruptions to pull him away. Now he needed to get both Erin and his non-Raleigh story idea out of his way. Erin he'd think about later.

Right now he was in the mood to write.

ERIN WOKE EARLY SATURDAY morning, earlier than usual and extremely early for not having gotten to bed until dawn. One thing was for certain. She would never look at The Daring Duo's table the same way again.

She was afraid, in fact, that every time she saw them sitting there she'd be tempted to pull them by the hair out of what she now considered *her* table. Hers and Sebastian's.

Dealing with what they'd done last night was going to take longer than four fairly sleepless hours. She certainly hadn't had the time or the energy to put anything into perspective once she'd arrived home. Having walked from the loft to the bar earlier in the evening, he'd accepted her offer of a lift since she was going his way.

She'd almost thought he'd decline, that he'd disappear into the city's shadows. But the ride up in the elevator was nothing like the one they'd shared the previous night. This time he'd said goodbye to her when the doors had opened on the sixth floor. Not with a kiss or any such intimate gesture, but with nothing more than one raised hand while he leaned against the back wall of the car.

She didn't know why she'd expected more; so what that they'd spent the past two hours engaged in mind-blowing sex? Having a Man To Do wasn't about sharing anything but their bodies. Sebastian seemed to have a better handle on that than she'd managed to grab thus far.

The four hours she had slept seemed to have been all the recharging time her brain needed. Her body still ached and craved another eight but her mind was racing, demanding she get her butt in gear. Still, before getting out of bed to brush her teeth or take care of the rest of her bathroom business, even before stumbling to the kitchen for the coffee, she did the one thing she had to do before she did anything else.

Unload on Tess and Samantha.

She dragged her laptop into her lap and began to type.

From: Erin Thatcher
Sent: Saturday
To: Samantha Tyler; Tess Norton
Subject: Screw Me Once? Shame On Me?

Okay, girls. I'm totally screwed. (Well, I've been totally screwed but that's another subject for another letter!)

You know all my talk of keeping emotions out of this affair with Sebastian? Uh-uh. Not happening.

Too late. I won't say I'm in love…but I'm definitely way over my head in like. So, what now?

He told me things last night. Things I'm still not certain are true. Things about his past that almost seemed to be a story made up for my benefit. To appease my curiosity, as it were, perhaps even to frighten me a bit so I'd quit wondering all the things I've been wondering and keep my mind and my heart from getting as involved as my body.

But the bone he threw me (ha!) totally backfired because he made me even more curious. And I couldn't exactly ask him to stop talking so I could find out if he was bullshitting me considering I was in a rather compromising position at the time. (How compromising, your nosy selves ask? <g> Let's just say there's a certain table in the bar I'll never again be able to look at with a straight face.)

And so my dilemma. Do I press him for the truth about what he told me? (I really do want to know!) Or do I just go with it, forget trying to figure out who he is and enjoy his company and his, uh, tongue? <g> I mean, right now, this moment, I could call this whole thing off and be able to look back with fond memories (she says, wondering as she does so if she's lying to herself). Yes, I'd miss the incredible sex.

But I'm afraid I'd miss Sebastian even more.

I guess I never did figure on wanting to get to know my Man To Do. (Stupid me!) There's even a part of me that has thought about ditching the sexual fling and seeing if we'd work out as friends. I think he'd really be interesting to know. More interesting to know even than fun to...well, you get the idea.

What do I do? ::whine, whine:: Erin

Not that she necessarily expected Tess or Samantha to have the perfect solution, but even a hint of what tack to take would help. As it was, Erin's mind might've been wound up into high gear, but it was a total wasteland when it came to any sort of cognizant decision-making.

Coffee. Then shower. Before anything else.

She headed to the kitchen, ground the last of her Sumatra beans, poured filtered water from the refrigerated jug into the coffeemaker and waited for the caffeine to brew. Double-size mug filled to the brim with the addition of sweetener and cream and she was on her way to being human.

She was also on her way to the shower, mug in one hand, towels in another, when her e-mail chime sounded, requiring a quick detour back to the bedroom. First things first. Waking up completely would have to wait another minute or two while she checked to see who had come through with much needed advice. Or the swift kick to the backside she deserved.

From: Tess Norton
Sent: Saturday
To: Erin Thatcher; Samantha Tyler
Subject: Re: Screw Me Once? Shame On Me?

Dear Erin:

Do exactly as I say. Do not deviate from this plan. Do this now:

1. Go to the nearest Starbucks
2. Order the Caramel Mocha Frappuccino

3. Also order the biggest chocolate brownie in the case

4. Sit down in a comfy chair to drink/eat

5. Ask yourself what's the worst that can happen with Sebastian?

6. Ask yourself what's the best that can happen with Sebastian?

7. Realize that NEITHER OF THOSE TWO THINGS ARE GOING TO HAPPEN! What will really happen is something you can neither anticipate nor prepare for.

THEREFORE:

1. Enjoy your coffee and brownie

2. Enjoy your time with Sebastian

3. Be true to your inner voice

4. Honor your libido

5. Don't play games—if you have a question, ask it

My, my, don't I sound wise? Sort of like Dr. Phill on estrogen. All kidding aside, I think the above is true. I think the key is the voice inside, and listening to it instead of making rationalizations for the things we want to listen to instead.

Not that I do that, mind you. I'm a moron and should be watched 24/7 by a team of psychiatrists. But that's another e-mail. I gotta run!

Love and kisses, Tess

Well, thought Erin, Tess was certainly on a roll this morning. She'd obviously been sniffing too much plant fertilizer if she thought she needed a psychiatrist. Tess had to be one of the most levelheaded women Erin had ever met—even if they'd only met in cyberspace.

She carried her mug to the shower, setting it on the ledge above the showerhead where she kept her shampoo and gel. Between the hot water and the hot coffee, she'd eventually get her body going. Curling back up in bed for another couple of hours sounded like a lot more fun than going to work. Curling back up in bed with Sebastian sounded even better.

But she had a party to plan. And no matter how much she'd rather do a half-dozen other things, including doing her Man To Do, she owed this one to Rory.

"I'VE BEEN TRYING TO GET Will to understand how Sebastian made up the story of The Daring Duo. Will thinks I'm exaggerating." Cali pouted. "I mean, I know I didn't hear all of what Sebastian was saying since I was working. But Will just doesn't believe that what I did hear was as cool as it was and it's totally pissing me off."

Cali's interruption of Erin's distracted musings was not the least bit unwelcome. She'd been wishing she'd followed Tess's advice and taken time for the Caramel Mocha Frappuccino and the brownie before coming to work, but she'd been thinking more about the party and less about her mental health.

All these hours later she was paying the price for that particular lapse in priorities. And the price tag kept getting higher. She'd think about the best thing that could happen with Sebastian then she'd think about the worst thing before starting the cycle all over again. For some reason she never could get to that place of nirvana halfway in between.

Yep. Two brownies would've been even better. A girl could never have too much chocolate. Whether or not she could have too much sex, or an adverse reaction to the sex she'd been having was something else altogether. Either Erin's long dormant hormones were bubbling against the lid of a pressure cooker—or else she was on the verge of succumbing to love at first sight. In this case, love at first sex.

"Exaggerating how?" Erin glanced from Cali to Will who was loading down his tray with frosted mugs and a pitcher of beer. Will's mouth was drawn into a tight grim line instead of into his usual boyish smile. Obviously Cali telling tales of their lover's spat did not sit well. For once Erin was on his side, the side of the one done wrong.

"Cali seems to think Sebastian has some sort of magical storytelling gift." Will hoisted up his tray. "I've been trying to convince her that there's nothing magic about telling a story. It's all about the elements and the way the author puts them together."

Erin's loyalties swung back to Cali. "Well, I don't know about an author's elements but I do know my granddad Rory could've given Hemingway a go. And Rory never put a word on paper. It was all in the way he told the tale."

Cali looked triumphant. Will looked just plain mad before walking away. Erin shrugged, not really wanting to get into the middle of what she was afraid was a personal problem between Cali and Will and their screenplay and not at all about Sebastian's storytelling skills.

Of course, they didn't know about the tale he'd woven last night while he'd had her spread open across The Daring Duo's table. The story that was giving Erin bloody hell today as she'd tried—unsuccessfully and all day long—to put what he'd said into any sort of perspective.

Or even into a context around which she could wrap either side of her brain. But logic wasn't working. Neither was her imagination. It was too far out there, the story he'd told. Little boys and little trucks and a cupcake begged from a bakery's back door.

"That's exactly what I'm talking about." Cali tossed a tray full of empties into the trash can designated for glass recycling. The bottles clattered loudly and Cali flinched before screwing up her face in apology. "Sorry."

Erin arched a brow. "You didn't learn anything from me taking out my frustration on the mugs the other night?"

With Will gone, Cali had room to speak freely. "Men are *so* aggravating. Everything has to be their way or the highway."

"Sometimes their way isn't such a bad thing." Erin glanced across the bar to the table where earlier she'd seated three female single twenty-somethings-seeking, unable to bear the thought of The Daring Duo defiling the table where she'd experienced Sebastian's firsthand knowledge of heaven.

"If you're being cheap and sleazy and talking about sex, then I agree. Having a man who knows what to do once he's got your clothes off is a beautiful thing." Before Erin could agree, Cali added, "But I hate it when they try to be an expert on everything and turn up their nose at even the hint—" she held forefinger and thumb a fraction of a millimeter apart "—the tiniest hint of a suggestion that they might be wrong. Or that another man might have the answer when they don't.''

Erin turned her attention to wiping down the bar. ''And this has to do with Sebastian how, exactly?''

Cali scrunched up both shoulders. ''Just that I told Will it might be kind of cool to see what Sebastian thought about our screenplay.''

Erin shook her head. ''I don't know, Cali. I'm not an expert on men, obviously,'' *what an understatement that was* ''but I can see where that might piss Will off. You wanting to get another man's input rather than trusting Will's intuition, especially when you two have just gotten started on what might really be a good relationship for the both of you.''

''Well, yeah. I can appreciate that.'' Smiling, Cali waved at a customer on his way out the door. ''I was just trying to find a way to save the screenplay for Will. This isn't about me or my grade or anything. This doesn't mean half as much to me as it does to Will. And I thought if he heard what I've been trying to tell him, but heard it from another guy instead of me, well, maybe he would listen.''

''Do what you have to do then, I guess.'' Erin's heart began to thump harder.

''Oh, thanks.'' Frowning, Cali grabbed two bottles from the cooler and sluiced ice from the labels with one hand. ''What kind of advice is that?''

''The only advice I can think of at the moment,'' Erin said because Sebastian had just walked through the door.

She was totally unprepared for the overwhelming emotion that hit her. She felt like *then,* before Sebastian, she'd only existed, and *now* she'd finally started to live. No matter how exciting her Man To Do adventure, that suggestion of having idly cruised through so many years didn't sit well. Especially coming on the heels of the plaguing doubts she'd been dodging here recently—doubts that had finally caught up with her.

If she were to be blunt, the entire situation sucked. The idea that she had only been drifting through life made a total mockery of the years spent learning the ropes with Rory, of the time she'd trekked across Europe on foot with the boy who'd been her first love, of the university credits she'd earned toward a degree she'd never declared.

Had she really spent her life in limbo? Waiting? For a man? The thought sent a wave of panic crashing like cymbals over her ears. This was just stress rearing its ugly head the way it did when she least needed the crushing reminder of all the things she had on her plate.

Oh, no. No way. This was getting ridiculous. A man was not the answer to her problems or her prayers. Certainly not Sebastian Gallo. That wasn't why he was here. She wiped her hands on her apron and turned to Cali. "I need to run to the little girls' room. Get Sebastian a beer and tell him I'll be right back, will you?"

"Sure, but don't you…"

Erin didn't hear the rest of what Cali had to say because the slamming of the office door drowned out her voice.

Count to thirty, Erin. Count to thirty.

Yes, she'd always known there was the possibility of involving her emotions, no matter how often she told herself not to let it happen. She was totally female, after all, and subject to all those niggling female anomalies like thinking on the heels of sex came love.

Grr and *grr* again. She banged her head back against the door on which she was leaning, then pushed off and finished the count to thirty while she crossed the small room. She dropped into her desk chair and, in desperate need of a distraction, pulled up her e-mail program, hoping Samantha had gotten around to answering this morning's pitiful cry for help.

And she had, bless her always timely heart. Willing her heart to calm its thundering pace, her blood pressure back to normal, her head to stop the pounding that was now echoing in her ears, Erin sat back to read.

From: Samantha Tyler
Sent: Saturday
To: Erin Thatcher; Tess Norton
Subject: Screw Me Once? Shame On Me?

Oh, Erin. Be careful. You don't really know all that much about Sebastian except that he's...ahem... talented. Make sure you're not mixing up "I love sex" with "I love you." A chick cliché!

Offhand I'd say forget being friends. If you guys have that much chemistry, there's no way you can back off from it and have that stick for more than...generous estimate? Twenty, thirty minutes.

I mean, think about it. Doesn't just looking into his eyes make you horny? I remember when I was falling in love with my ex, even his dandruff made me horny. (Okay, that was over the top, but you know what I mean). And you think you can be his buddy?

(Samantha shakes her head vigorously and makes that tsk-tsk noise that is *so* annoying.)

Friendship plus sex equals love. If you think there's potential for a future together, then stick it out. If not, run like hell. That kind of heartbreak no one needs, and the longer you wait, the deeper you get in, the worse it hurts.

The middle ground? Keep your mouth shut unless it's giving pleasure, your ears closed to any of his human side, and leave your heart at home? Nice idea, but no. Never works. If you're falling in love, that's not going to stop the slide, no matter how much you tell yourself it will.

I hate to sound negative. And remember, my divorce is probably making me a bitter, cynical hag before my time. I would love, love, *love* you to have a happy ending with this guy, but what are the odds?

Remember, you picked him out because he's so wrong for you! I wish Tess and I could meet the guy! Samantha

P.S. So what the hell *is* all this stuff you're finding out about his past that you're hinting at and driving us crazy by not telling? What was he, a mafia hit man? Drug lord? CIA? Salad prep at the Chew and Chat?

The Chew and Chat? Oh, good grief. Erin chuckled, then sighed, then shook her head. That Samantha was a piece of work—not to mention the perfect diversion. She'd also made more than a few points that gave Erin pause. *Friendship plus sex equals love.* The sentiment made so much sense, as did the rest of what Samantha had said.

So where into her equation did Erin's feelings for Sebastian fall? Serious like. Definite infatuation. A truly consuming lust. All things that fit with a relationship's adrenaline beginnings. But this was not a relationship. Or even the beginning of one. She didn't even know if anything she'd learned about Sebastian was real.

She'd gone into this affair looking for relief—from work stress and her worries about disappointing Rory, not to mention her horny hormones. All she'd accomplished was a temporary appeasing of the latter. Because every time she saw him she wanted him more than the time before.

She rubbed at the thundering, pounding, blood pressure headache. It was so simple really. All she needed was a light at the end of the tunnel, the tiniest ray of sunshine filtering down through the murky water of her mind. That wasn't asking too much, was it? To know she wouldn't spend the rest of her life feeling so decidedly out of sorts?

A sharp rap sounded on her door and, before she could decide whether or not to answer, Sebastian walked into the room. She swallowed hard, wishing for an analgesic. Better yet, a margarita, hold the salt. Hold the lime. Hell, hold everything but the tequila.

His gaze on hers, he shut the door behind him. And even from where she sat on the other side of the desk, Erin felt the reverberation.

9

"ARE YOU AVOIDING ME?"

Not in the way he was implying. She hadn't run because she didn't want to see him again. Quite the contrary. But, yes. For the moment she thought it best to work out her emotional conflict alone. "What? Can't a girl take a bathroom break without coming under suspicion?"

One darkly arched brow went up but his mouth remained...not grim, but certainly unsmiling. He crossed his arms over his chest and leaned back against the door. "Is that what you're doing?"

She gave a one-shouldered shrug, inclined her head toward the private office bathroom. Nonchalance came at a huge price to her stomach that burned as if she'd picked up a six-pack of ulcers. "I haven't made it yet. I stopped to check on an e-mail I was expecting."

"And now you're thinking about how to respond?"

How did he manage to remain so coolly detached when she was on a razor's edge of coming undone? "Actually, I'm thinking about what I read, trying to decide if it helped my current dilemma."

"You have a dilemma?"

"A bit of one," she admitted, striving for the objectivity she'd never find as long as he stood in the room, her night creature who should've been uncomfortable in the confining space of her office but managed to look totally at ease while she simmered and stewed.

And then it hit her, that this was all wrong. He should've been the one pacing while she sat back calmly and watched. This was her turf, her place to work while he walked the streets, doing the thinking that apparently kept him up all hours for whatever reason he hadn't bothered to share. He was the source of her agitation, his seeming unflappability in the face of an involvement making her insane.

She wanted to see if she could rile him up, scare him away, make him pay for part of what she was feeling. Elbows propped on the arms of her chair, she laced her hands over her midsection and lifted her chin. "You're my dilemma."

"You don't say."

"I do say. It's quite inconvenient actually, you see, because every time I'm near you I want to take off my clothes. No wait." She held up a hand when he started to speak. "That's not exactly right. Every time I see you, I want *you* to take off my clothes."

"And that's a bad thing?"

She had to give him credit. He'd actually managed to keep a straight face. "You tell me."

"C'mon, Erin. I'm a guy." His gaze grew piercing, intense, finally revealing that he was not unaffected. "What do you think I'm going to say?"

I want you to say what you're feeling, not what you're thinking, and not some obvious male cliché. "I guess I just want you to be honest."

"You want me to be honest." Lips pressed tight, he nodded while he thought it over, then lifted a brow and asked, "You want me to tell you that when I see your eyes light up I get hard?"

She blinked, tried to remember how to breathe. Why, oh, why did he have to say things like that? It was all she could do to keep her gaze from dropping from his face to his groin. "If that's your honesty. Then, yeah. Feel free."

"It is honest. And it is real. And, yeah." He huffed out a breath of self-directed ire, looked away, looked back. "It's been that way for more than a few months."

A few months? So…the initial sense of mutual attraction hadn't been her imagination? And this affair wasn't as out of the blue, as crazy as she'd thought? But it was an affair, wasn't it? No matter who had been the one to make the first move, what they were doing here now was all about the chemistry of bodies—not that existing between souls.

It wasn't even friendship. She had no idea what he did for a living, where he ate his favorite food, what the hell his favorite food might be. He liked champagne and books and showers and got hard when he looked into her eyes.

"A few months ago, huh? That's when I moved into the lofts." She waited for him to answer the question she hadn't really asked. To admit that she was his distraction. That he shared even a fraction of her fixation and fascination that they'd come together the way they had.

All he did was push away from the door and walk toward her. "I know exactly when you moved in. And I'd really gotten used to living alone."

He circled her desk and Erin's heart pitter-pattered as he moved to block the only path from her chair to the door. She swiveled to face him—and face her fears—head-on. She wanted the truth. What did she have to do with the reality that he *did* live alone?

He leaned his backside against the edge of the credenza that turned her L-shaped desk into a horseshoe. Wrapping his hands over the edge of the dark wood on either side of his hips, he stretched out his legs. His gaze held hers with no effort at all. She was right; he was a magician. And she was totally under his spell.

He wore black denim and biker boots, and crossed his ankles at the ends of his very long legs. His V-neck sweater was rich chocolate brown and tonight the growth of beard on his face was later than a five o'clock shadow and added to an aura just this side of menacing.

She refused to allow the intimidation. "You still live alone."

He shook his head. "No. You live there. Not physically, but you're there. And I have hell going to sleep. Forget what you've done to my ability to concentrate on work. Or now what you've done to my showers."

"Showers you take alone." It hit her then, what he was saying. His fantasies had been on a par with hers…yet they'd been different. They'd been more.

Slowly, she pushed out of her chair, braced her body against her desk, facing him in a mirror to his pose, the toes of her shoes touching the soles of his boots. He left his feet where they were, giving her the encouragement to continue. "You do more than shower alone, don't you?"

He didn't shrug off her comment, which meant she'd hit a bull's-eye of sorts, a target she wasn't sure he was aware of giving her with his admission that he couldn't shake her off as easily as he might have wanted to do.

She waited patiently, as patiently as she could manage with curiosity eating her up, and was finally rewarded when he blew out a breath of surrender, telling her almost as much with that sigh as he did with the words that followed.

"Well, I don't have family. I work at home. My business contacts are long-distance for the most part. No close friends, or at least none living here. So, yeah. I eat alone. Sleep alone." A corner of his mouth lifted. "Walk the streets alone."

"And you have sex alone."

She waited for the denial, the resentful response to the implied insult she'd cast upon his masculinity. The "how dare she suggest" he made do with his own right hand because he couldn't get a woman into bed. Funny how quickly she forgot who she was dealing with.

None of his reactions to the things she'd said or done had ever been remotely similar to the responses of other men she'd known. Why did she think this time would be any different? Whoever Sebastian Gallo was, he was secure in himself, in the way he lived his life, in the choices he made defining his existence.

The air in the room grew heavy and still, thick with the tension left uncut between them. Neither one of them moved; both remained standing, staring, cross-purposes like an invisible web of motion sensors keeping them apart. The whir of the computer's fan hummed in the background, and Erin swore she could hear the tic of the vein in his temple.

The face-off continued, the strain more about untold revelations, about Sebastian giving up a part of himself he wasn't ready to share, than it was about anything sexual. Yet, the picture of Sebastian in his shower, alone and in the throes of self-satisfaction stirred Erin beyond belief.

"Having sex alone has been known to happen."

"As can be said of most men. But you're not most men." A fact of which she'd be eternally grateful, no matter how much further they took this affair.

For now, however, she was more interested in taking this conversation to a place where she could find her answers. "You said you don't have any family. Have you ever been married?"

He shook his head. "Never."

"Relationships?" She arched a brow and added, "Old girlfriends who keep you company when you get the urge?"

"The urge to do what?" He moved, but only to cross his arms over his chest. "Have sex that doesn't involve the shower, the soap and my right hand?"

She did her best not to smile. "It's been known to happen."

"Not with old girlfriends, though."

"With who, then?" she asked, pressing forward.

"With girls—" He stopped, corrected his misstep. "With women, who happen to be friendly when I stop by."

"When's the last time you stopped?" She didn't know why this was important, only that curiosity demanded she ask.

"I don't know," he answered without missing a beat.

"You don't know the last time you slept with a woman?" He had to be bullshitting her. "Isn't that something most guys notch on their bedpost?"

"I'm not most guys."

Okay. She knew that. She also knew most guys would lie through their teeth before opening themselves up with that sort of admission. And if he was being truthful about the sex he hadn't been having before having it with her… "So, the story you told me last night? About living in the abandoned building? That was the truth?"

One, two, three heartbeats passed before he nodded once and said, "As raw as it gets."

Her heart shattered into pieces she was sure she'd never put together again. She buried her face in her hands. "You can't do this to me. You can't tell me that you don't have family or friends. That you live alone and work alone. That you have sex alone."

"Why not, Erin? It's my life. Not yours. I don't dwell on any of that. It's who I am."

She waved her hands frantically. "No, no, no. You told me that you can't sleep because I'm there. How am I supposed to respond to that when I know that you're so truly alone?"

How terribly he must've been hurt as a child. A hurt he denied, a hurt she couldn't even imagine resulting from a truth so horrible she almost wished he'd told her his words were a lie.

"Alone, Erin. Not lonely. And I never said I didn't want you there."

Erin waited, looking into his eyes, knowing that couldn't possibly be all of what he had to say. But his mouth had drawn into a thinly pressed line…his mouth that she'd only kissed that night in the mailroom. How could she not have realized that they'd never kissed again?

Why had he never kissed her again?

The office door burst open. Sebastian's head came up. Erin jumped to her feet and whirled around. Cali stood in the doorway and wore the panicked look of a gunshot victim waiting to fall.

Erin's pulse raced. "What is it? What's going on?"

Cali's eyes grew even wider. "Erin you are not going to believe what Will just found out about Courtland's."

CREWE COURTLAND, THE NEW jazz café down the street from Paddington's, had announced their mid-November grand opening date weeks ago. What they hadn't made public until tonight, or until last night since it was now the wee hours of Sunday morning, was their pre-grand opening.

On Halloween night.

Paddington's anniversary night.

Erin's night.

Sebastian felt the urge to drive his fist into the mouth of the nearest trumpet or sax.

He couldn't put his finger on the reason why, but he had a feeling word of Erin's party plans had leaked—in which case his fist would make more of an impact connecting with the jaw of the suspect ex-employee. But he kept his suspicions—and his thoughts of violence—to himself. He needed to consider Erin's needs, not his own. Though, lately, he'd found it difficult to differentiate between the two.

Strange, but coming to grips with that reality hadn't been as hard as he'd thought.

Along with Cali and Will, Sebastian had come home with Erin after the bar had closed. The late hours didn't bother him and he knew Erin was used to being up half the night. How the other two managed he had no idea. But he was glad the couple had been there for Erin.

After the intensity of the encounter earlier in her office where, having finally come to accept the truth of the past that he'd lived, she'd nearly fallen apart, Sebastian had a feeling he and Erin wouldn't have made much headway toward a reasonable resolution to her problem.

But with Cali and Will as buffers, the four of them together had come up with a workable list of options to make sure Erin's anniversary party didn't put her in the red. Not that a single option on the list would have the impact of what Sebastian was going to do.

What he had to do—and would do for the reasons and the feelings he'd been fighting since the day they'd met. Reasons he'd refused to give credence because it shouldn't have mattered that a woman he hardly knew was on the verge of losing her business. Feelings he'd refused to give life because loving her increased the risk to the only way he knew to survive.

Yet, Erin losing her business did matter, and tied into the primal response of a man's need to protect his woman. If only they'd met at a different time, a different place. Too many obstacles remained for him to voice his true feelings—obstacles he saw no way to overcome. His entire career depended on maintaining his solitary existence. Yet Erin was about to lose the career she'd worked her entire life to build.

Even counting the personal cost, the loss to his anonymity, how could he not intervene?

For some reason during the foursome's brainstorming session, Erin's concerns about Paddington's had returned over and again to her grandfather. Sebastian hadn't yet figured that out. He hoped to get some kind of answer here shortly. Which was why he was sitting in her window seat, one leg stretched the length of the padded cushion, one foot dragging the floor.

Will had left earlier claiming the need for sleep. Cali, whose wistful gaze had followed him out the door, was still in the kitchen with Erin helping to wash up the group's wineglasses and ashtrays. None of them smoked, but tonight it had seemed like the thing to do. Erin especially. Her stress level had finally mellowed.

Though Sebastian pitched in an idea or two here and there, he'd been a lot more interested in people watching. The dynamics of these three people in particular and especially how Cali and Will had both rallied around Erin as if they shared in the fate of Paddington's.

What they shared in was the fate of Erin. The same trap Sebastian had unwittingly fallen into.

Interesting concept, friendship. He didn't write about it a lot because Raleigh didn't have friends. He had co-workers and informants the same way Sebastian had an agent, an editor and a publicist, as well as an attorney and financial planner. These were the associates with whom he "did lunch."

He didn't have anyone to help him pull a party or a plot out of the toilet. Richie had died ten years ago, but he'd never quit harping on Sebastian's insistence on remaining a recluse. The aging inmate had badgered Sebastian every time he'd visited. Richie never had liked the way Sebastian kept to himself. Seeing him get involved with Erin and the others would've had the old man cackling.

It rather had Sebastian laughing at the irony. Richie had always said a woman would be the one to take Sebastian down in the end. He'd never believed it, of course. Nothing to do with his mother abandoning him in the first place and having any sort of impenetrable heart. It was just that vow he'd taken all those years ago to never rely on another human being for safety, sustenance or support.

For the most part he'd included sex in the equation and had made do with his shower. For the most part, because once in a while he'd allowed himself the need of women. He'd admitted as much to Erin, but hadn't been totally honest. Had, in fact, evaded answering her direct question about the last time he'd had sex.

He didn't plan to give her an answer because, quite frankly, it wasn't any of her business. But that was the short meaningless response. The truth was that he didn't want to think about sex that hadn't meant anything when it was beginning to mean a lot with Erin.

He pushed open her window, listening to the silence of the city, realizing this was exactly where she sat when he was thinking of her from one floor above. That this room was where she slept when he restlessly paced upstairs.

His pacing of late was even beginning to get on his own nerves because it meant his concentration level was shot. And he really doubted fantasies of Erin would cut any mustard with his publisher's legal department when he turned in this manuscript late.

Even if it felt like the best work he'd ever done. And even if he knew he had to take the chance on the new direction his writing seemed to be headed these days thanks to his muse.

Damn the bitch for making a mess of his life.

And damn himself for seeing no way out.

CALI PULLED HER Focus out of Erin's parking garage at 4:00 a.m. and headed home. Considering the hour and the last four nights' combined lack of sleep, logic said she should be exhausted. She was anything but. In fact, she was totally jazzed.

After Will had left the emergency brainstorming session earlier, Cali had managed to snag a bit of Sebastian's time while Erin dozed. Leaving with Will would've been Cali's preference, but she couldn't go until she'd helped Erin wash up the few dishes they'd used. Or without making sure Erin was going to be okay.

Besides, Will hadn't asked.

At first, Cali had pouted. Then she realized Will's being gone meant she and the screenplay were alone with Sebastian. She couldn't have planned it better. While Erin had fitfully napped, Cali had tucked her feet up on the sofa and pitched her idea to Sebastian sitting at the opposite end. He'd listened, but he'd kept one eye on Erin curled up on the love seat at his side. And that was okay. In fact, Cali found his divided attention endearingly cute.

In hushed tones, Cali had explained to Sebastian the version of the screenplay she and Will had on paper, and had then gone on to share her personal vision of the story idea. Sebastian had agreed with all but one of the possibilities she'd tossed out. And then he'd given her more input on crafting a plot than she'd ever expected. In fact, she'd walked out of Erin's building with her brain reeling.

Never in her life had she wished for a mini-tape recorder more than she did during the drive home. As it was, she'd headed out of downtown with the light over her rearview mirror trained down on the passenger seat where, one eagle eye on the near-empty road, she'd jotted notes on her ever-present, letter-size, legal pad.

An amazing night's work, she thought, finally turning into the narrow driveway separating the two squat buildings that made up her tiny apartment complex in midtown. A dozen efficiencies for like-minded cheap-skates and starving student waitresses. One of these days, with the right screenplay in hand...oh, yeah. She'd be moving uptown. And she could hardly wait.

She cut the car's engine, keeping the light on while she scribbled down several thoughts still fresh in her mind. A sharp rap on the passenger glass sent thoughts, pencil and pad skittering. Her hand flew to her throat, then to her heart. Nerves fired from eyes to brain and she finally registered Will's face. A deep breath later, she hit the door locks and Will dropped into the passenger seat.

She backhanded his upper arm, once, twice, a third time for good measure. "You scared the crap outta me."

"I figured you saw my car. You parked right beside me." He rubbed at his newly bruised shoulder.

"Well, I didn't. It's dark and my mind was... elsewhere." She reached back for her tote bag in the floorboard behind her seat, hoping to stash the legal pad before Will noticed exactly where her mind had been. "What're you doing here anyway? I thought you were tired."

"I was. I am." He shrugged and then he smiled. "I couldn't sleep. I've gotten too used to you tucking me in."

Cali wanted to revel in the sweet feelings inspired by his admission; it had been so long since a man had cared the way Will cared, accepting her, wanting her. Loving her with his body even if he hadn't put the feelings into words.

But her bag was caught up beneath her seat and she feared his discovery of her betrayal. At least what he would consider a betrayal. She considered what she was doing exactly what a good student would do.

"Grr. Stupid bag," she muttered and tugged harder.

Will leaned toward her, reached back and freed the tote. Handing it to her with one hand, he reached up and tucked a curl behind her ear with the other. "That's okay. You don't have to tuck me in if you're not in the mood."

"It's not that." His touch made this that much harder. She glanced furtively at the pad before stuffing it down in her tote, knowing as she did that she'd just given herself away.

Will followed the direction of her gaze, frowned and slid the pad back out. He scanned her hastily made notes. "What's all this?"

"Nothing really." She shrugged. "A few ideas I was thinking about on the way home."

"Hmm." He continued to read, frowning, snorting, shaking his head. "I don't think this is nothing, Cali. I think this is you going behind my back." Another couple of minutes of study and he handed her back the legal pad, as if daring her to deny what was so plainly scribbled in blue ink on yellow.

So, she faced the charge. "You left. Erin was half-asleep on the sofa. So, Sebastian and I got to talking."

Will nodded as if he didn't believe a word she said. "And the subject of the screenplay just happened to come up?"

Cali shifted in her seat to better face him. "No, I brought it up. I told you I was thinking of running the idea by Sebastian. I don't know why you're so surprised."

"I guess I shouldn't be." He slouched defensively

in the corner of the seat, his back against the door. "Nothing I've had to say has mattered so far."

"Bullshit," Cali blurted, shocking even herself. "This is a joint project and has been since the beginning. That doesn't mean it's perfect."

"I never said it was perfect." He jerked his glasses from his face and rubbed at his eyes. "What I said was that I didn't see any reason to ask Sebastian's opinion."

"And I told you that I did. That I thought his input might be worthwhile. Or interesting at least." Cali took a deep breath, working to dispel her aggravation before it turned into anger. "I haven't known too many people able to tell a story off the cuff the way he can."

"This is so friggin' ridiculous." Will shoved his glasses back in place and hooked his fingers over the door handle. "I can't believe I'm having to put up with this crap."

She wanted to say "ditto" because Will was dishing out crap based on nothing more than hurt feelings. At least her "crap" came from a desire to do right by the screenplay. "Do you want to find a new study partner then?"

"What good will that do this late in the semester? Like we can split the screenplay?" He bit off a curse and instead added a terse, "Right. I can see that happening."

Which meant if he could find a way to do just that, he would. Cali knew well how to listen to what he wasn't saying as clearly as she heard what he did.

She finished shoving the legal pad into her tote bag. "So, if we're this diametrically opposed to our story approach, where do we go from here?"

He faced her then, his brown-gold eyes glittering in

the car's bright interior light. A tic jerked at his jawline beneath the stubble that added to his look of weary indignation. "I don't know. Why don't you tell me?"

She was not giving up on this. She was not. "I don't know about you, but I'm going inside. I'm going to sleep. And, when I get up, I'm going to work on incorporating what I can of my notes into the screenplay."

She wondered if he remembered that, yesterday, she'd brought home his laptop. If he took the computer back, he'd make her effort that much harder. Right now, she wouldn't put it past him. "I just want to see if these ideas work before I toss them off as fodder."

"What? You mean there's a chance the great Sebastian Gallo doesn't know his head from a hole in the ground?"

Cali frowned. "Are you jealous? Of Sebastian?"

"Jealous?" Will sputtered. "Try again."

Cali shrugged, hoisted her tote strap over her shoulder. "I can't. I'm clueless."

"You're right. You are clueless." He pushed open the door and climbed from the car. Cali followed suit, hitting the automatic locks and staring at Will across the car's roof. She did her best to ignore what he'd said, to put it into context, but the hurt lingered.

The interior light faded, leaving them in darkness but for the streetlamp at the driveway's entrance. Will shoved a hand back over his already mussed hair. "No, Cali. I'm not jealous. I'm angry. I'm pissed in a very big way. I don't see this as the way a partnership works. That one half does what she wants over the objections of the other."

"I know how a partnership works, Will." And even as she said it, she knew she was adding a deeper subtext to their own personal plot. "It's a hashing out of joint ideas and, yes, the exploration of individual ones. This doesn't mean any changes I make will end up in the finished project. But I have to do this. For me. I have to know if my intuition is right."

"Sebastian's intuition you mean."

"No. My intuition. My ideas. Sebastian was nothing but a sounding board. He was open-minded. And he listened." Cali paused and, before fully thinking her comment through, she added, "That's the least I expect in a partnership."

Will remained silent, his fingertips drumming on the roof of her car. His mouth thinned into a grim line. His eyes went flat. Cali felt the first stirrings of big-mouth regret deep in the pit of her stomach.

"Fine," Will finally said. "Whatever. You do what you have to do. I'll do the same." He turned and headed for his car, calling back over his shoulder, "Bring my laptop to class on Monday. I'm going to need it."

10

AT THE SOUND OF THE bedroom door closing, Sebastian looked up. Erin, exhausted, leaned back against it, still wearing the head-to-toe black Paddington's uniform that looked like no uniform he'd ever seen when she wore it. Her complexion was more pale than usual, the circles under her eyes darker than he thought he'd ever seen.

But she was still an incredibly gorgeous creature and his groin tightened in response. The sensation was one he'd grown to expect and embrace. But the same sort of tightening that clutched at his chest was new, not particularly welcome, and a feeling he had no intent to explore.

At least not now, tonight, this morning. Not when his current agenda involved more closely examining what was going on with Erin, not with himself. He'd done way too much of that already the last few days. And he was more than uncomfortable with the conclusions he'd reached.

He shut the window and got to his feet, crossing the room and silently taking Erin by the hand. He led her to the foot of the bed where he faced her, tugged her polo shirt from the waistband of her pants and off over her head.

She didn't say a word, didn't object by expression or body language, even when he released the clasp of her bra and freed her breasts. All she did in return was lift the hem of his sweater and pull it over his head.

Her hands found their way to his shoulders and she slowly dragged her palms down his chest, circling her fingertips over his nipples then pushing into his armpits and laying her head gently on his chest.

He wasn't about to deny his arousal but right now it meant next to nothing compared to Erin's needs. Leaving the briefest kiss on his sternum, she moved her hands to the fastenings of his pants. He reciprocated and both pulled off shoes and socks and skinned pants down legs until wearing nothing but practical black cotton underwear of the same cut they'd been wearing the first time they'd shared this intimacy.

But this time their bare skin was more about baring souls than bodies and that realization hit Sebastian hard. So hard he wondered for a moment where and how he'd been so weak as to let her get to him as she obviously had. Erin backed away and moved to douse all the room's light but for the single bedside lamp. She pulled back the quilt and crawled beneath, pleading with her gaze for him to follow.

And so he did, stretching out his much longer legs and tucking the quilt around her shoulders, tucking her weary body spoon-fashion back into his. They lay that way for at least five minutes, sinking into the pillows and mattress, bodies adjusting to being together in bed, hands here, feet there, legs working in and out of one another until their breathing settled into a matching rhythm, their chests rising as one.

"I can't believe I'm this exhausted," Erin said, her voice barely above a whisper.

"You've had a lot going on lately. Work, planning your party." He hesitated, added, "Me."

She didn't say anything and he wasn't sure if she wasn't listening, if she agreed, or if she was weighing options for easing her stress load. He would be the easiest to get rid of and the first to go. As well he should be.

And being long ago done with any abandonment issues he'd once battled, he wasn't quite sure why the thought of her kicking him out left him ill at ease.

"I've put so much effort into this celebration. How the hell is Paddington's supposed to compete when Courtland's is bringing in the jazz talent most fans have to pay big bucks to hear?" She sighed but her body had already grown tense. "Half the time I don't even know why I bother."

He didn't know her well but what he did know assured him she wasn't a defeatist. "It's not a bother. It's your life."

She shook her head against the pillow and against his chest. "It was my granddad's life. My life is..."

She let the sentence trail and he wondered if she really didn't know or have an answer. He placed his hand on her hip and she moved closer to his body, if closer were truly possible considering he could already feel her bones where the curve of her spine pressed his torso.

"I grew up with Rory, my granddad. He raised me after my parents died. I was eleven and Rory gave up his entire life in Devon and moved here so I wouldn't have to be uprooted."

Sebastian rubbed her hip, up and down in a soothing motion to work out what tightness he could from her muscles. He adjusted his other arm beneath his head on the pillow and nuzzled his chin on the top of Erin's head.

She exhaled a bone deep sigh. "Rory did so much for me and you would think the least I could do for him would be to carry on with what was the joy of his life."

Strange thing to say. "Isn't that what you're doing?"

"I suppose so, but in case you haven't noticed there isn't a lot of joy involved for me."

Actually, he hadn't noticed that at all. What he'd seen he had chalked up to the normal stress of running a business, not dissatisfaction at feeling stuck in the life. He gave a small shrug, wondering exactly whether she considered the bar hers at all, or whether she still thought of it as Rory's. "So, sell the bar. Do what you want to do with your life."

"I don't know what I want to do with my life," was all she said.

But it was the way she said it, the exhaustion that went beyond the need for sleep, a tiredness that spoke of a weary soul that clutched hard in the region of Sebastian's heart. He didn't want to feel the need to set things right, or the urge to soothe whatever he could of her emotional ache. A few things, however, he couldn't control.

Funny how they both seemed to be at a crisis point. His had been a nagging pain in the ass now for several months, rearing her annoying little head every time he sat down with Raleigh to write. He wondered… "You've been running Paddington's for a year?"

She nodded again. "Rory died three years ago. Once his estate was settled, I worked with a designer on the remodeling of the bar. We reopened last October."

He continued to rub her hip, over the cotton of her panties to the smooth skin of her thigh. "Before he died. What were you doing then?"

She snorted. "Nothing. Everything. I traveled. I took university classes. I have way too many credits for someone with no degree. I thought about declaring business as my major because Rory was always asking my advice, which was a totally ridiculous ploy to get me involved in the running of the bar. He'd been in business longer than I'd been alive."

"You had money from your parents, then."

"Oodles. Ridiculous, really. All the money to do what I wanted and I never knew what I wanted to do."

He thought about that for several minutes, his hand moving to Erin's waist and rubbing there and down over her belly. He'd known for as long as he could remember what he wanted to do. Hell, he'd made up stories when pushing that little yellow truck through the ashes of dead fires.

Richie had been the one to help prep Sebastian for college when the visiting counselor had shot him down, telling him he'd be wasting his time to aim beyond trade school. He'd aimed way, way beyond and had put himself through the five years it had taken to earn his four-year degree.

Five more years and his first book was in the publication pipeline. He'd found his niche, but he still wasn't satisfied, greedy bastard that he was, wanting more.

Erin rolled over onto her stomach and propped up on her elbows. The plump side of one breast pressed against his ribs. Her eyes glittered and her gaze probed. "What are you thinking?"

He couldn't tell her. Writing was a part of his life he didn't share. Even being here with her now, this way, talking about life and dreams. He was growing too complacent, too comfortable, and he stiffened rather than answer.

Erin grew pensive, obviously sensing his backing away. "Do I frighten you somehow? Are you afraid I'm going to tie you up and torture you free of your secrets?"

Sebastian rolled over onto his back, crossed his arms behind his head. "Torture away. I don't have any secrets."

Erin's grin said give-me-a-break with more sarcasm than her voice. "What're you talking about? Everything about you is a secret. You haven't told me anything about who you are or what you do or things you've done in your life."

He stared into her eyes, watching the low-burning lamplight draw silver flecks from pure hazel. Her nose was long and straight, her mouth lush, her lips plump in the way a man enjoyed. He felt an urge to cup the back of her head and pull her mouth to his.

An urge he forced himself to resist even while forcing a retreat from the intimacy she sought. Safety, sustenance and support. He needed no one to give him any of those things. What Erin looked ready to offer went totally off his radar and he had no choice but to push her away.

"Is that what I'm here for? That's what you want? To know everything about me?" When she didn't answer, when she continued to meet his gaze without blinking, he added, "I didn't think what we were doing required more than what we already know."

Her expression remained unchanged though the softness paled and what he could only imagine was hope faded away.

"You're right," she finally said. "There's not a thing you could tell me that would make any difference to why we're here."

He waited, tensed, expecting any minute for her to ask him to leave. So, when instead, a minute later, she moved closer and climbed up to straddle his lower body, all he could do was close his eyes, let her have her way and play the part of the convenient dick.

Not that doing so required much effort. Certainly not the same effort required to ignore how right this felt because this was Erin sliding down his body and not some nameless female or even one who'd mentioned her name before rolling on his condom.

He tensed further, told himself to relax. Impossible, because Erin brushed her lips down the center of his torso and dipped her tongue in and out of his navel. She nipped at the surrounding skin, tiny bites with the edges of her teeth followed by a soothing bath from her tongue.

Blood pooled heavily in his groin and he held himself still when he wanted more than anything to surge upward. Her bare breasts plumped against the tops of his thighs and her hands at his hips held fast.

She moved lower, her teeth, lips and tongue toying with the waistband of his boxer briefs where it rode low on his abs and behind which his erection strained. When she drew one finger from the head of his dick to the base, Sebastian gave up all attempts to stay aloof and groaned from the center of his gut.

He spread his legs, knowing if this was going to go where he wanted her to take it, his shorts had to go. He lifted his hips; Erin shoved him back down, keeping a hand flat on his stomach. *A woman in charge.* He liked the concept, liked it a lot. He'd let her be the boss as long as she didn't stop what she was doing, blowing hot air through her open mouth down the same trail her finger had followed.

Her fingertips slipped beneath the elastic—finally— and she eased down the band, but only far enough to expose the head of his dick which she summarily took into her mouth to suck. He huffed out several short breaths and this time it was Erin who pulled off his shorts when he lifted his hips and begged.

She took him fully into her mouth. He hit the back of her throat and felt her lips wrap around the base of his shaft. *Unbelievable.* He hated to move, to dilute the sensation, but when she pressed her most intimate kiss around him and pulled upward, he followed, thrusting because she made it impossible to do anything less.

She wrapped her hand around his erection and held him still. Her mouth moved up and down, her tongue swirled over the head, her lips caught the ridge where sensation centered. Her hold tightened, the pressure and the rhythm of her mouth increased.

And then she slid her other hand between his legs, stroking behind his balls and finding the source of his building pressure. She pushed hard, pushed harder. He groaned and she took her exploration lower, fingering him in places he most wanted her touch.

But he was going to come and this wasn't what he wanted. He wanted to be buried as deep in her body as size and position allowed. "Erin," he grunted, his voice hoarse and ragged.

She released him, her hands and her mouth moving back up his torso, tickling and teasing until, still wearing her panties, she straddled him. Her smiling face hovered inches over his.

"Damn you, woman. Tell me you have a condom."

Her smile widened and she reached into the drawer of her bedside table and handed him the packet. She worked herself out of her panties while he worked himself into the latex. And then she positioned her body above his and lowered herself completely.

He couldn't stand it. He couldn't handle anything else that was slow and easy. He wanted her now and he flipped her over, driving his body deeply into hers. Fingernails scraped down his back. Heels urged him forward, digging into his backside, her long legs moving up to wrap around his waist. She cried out. It hadn't even been a minute and she came. He continued thrusting, driving, pumping into her.

His orgasm consumed him. There was no other word for the overpowering sensation of being ripped in half, burned alive, torn apart from everything safe he'd ever known. He couldn't wait to come down, to finish, to be free of her hold. He pulled out, rolled up to sit on the edge of the bed.

For a moment all he had the strength to do was sit, elbows on his knees, face buried in his hands. Sit and breathe and do what he could to pull himself back together. He felt Erin turn toward him, felt the touch of her hand to his back and, before she had the chance to call out his name, he left the bed.

Once in the bathroom, he pulled off the condom and flushed. And then he looked into the mirror. And he didn't like anything about the man looking back. The man who lived alone for a reason and had known the first time he'd crushed his mouth to Erin's that he was making a huge mistake.

He'd abandoned every one of life's lessons for what he'd tried to tell himself was nothing but a great piece of ass, when the reality was that he was in over his head, far beneath his comfort zone of emotion with no possibility of ever surfacing for air. Taking her down with him only furthered his sensation of strangling. Which was why he would save her.

But then he would destroy her.

There was nothing else he could do.

ERIN NEVER WENT TO THE bar on Sunday. Never, because Sunday was her one and only completely free personal day of the week. She'd promised herself never to do more than attend church and buy groceries. The rest of the day was for shopping or the movies or anything else she deemed fun.

But here she was, unlocking the back door into the bar having walked the several blocks from the loft. She'd woken with an insane headache and spent too long in the shower trying to steam it away. The shower, in fact, only doubled the pain's intensity because the ache spread down her neck, over her shoulders, and wove a web around her heart.

The resulting nausea had convinced her to skip buying groceries—who could eat when on the verge of vomiting? And, since she'd already missed church, she figured she might as well use the time to catch up on Paddington's accounting, having slacked off the last three nights.

She turned on the lights and the ceiling fan low to

stir the still air. Dropping into her desk chair, she wondered if Tess and Samantha were tired of her yet. She opened her e-mail program but hesitated before starting a new message, waiting while the usual spam mail and Eve's Apple digests filled her inbox.

Erin groaned. She was *so* behind on reading Anaïs Nin. No doubt the group had already discussed *Little Birds*—which she hadn't picked up since reading those few pages after work on Wednesday night—and moved on to *Delta of Venus*. If she didn't get busy and participate, she'd lose her spot in the queue for choosing the next author, and she was determined to introduce the group to Emma Holly's erotica.

Neither Tess nor Sam had said a word about the goings-on with Eve's Apple, but she hadn't thought to ask, being so caught up sending them her Man To Do missives. She hated whining to her cyber-girlfriends as much as she hated whining to Cali. Besides, Tess and Sam would both be well within their rights to give her a big fat, "I told you so."

Not only had Erin *not* gone to Starbucks for a brownie and a Frappuccino à la Tess, she'd also stupidly done all the things Samantha had warned her not to do. Especially the worst offender. The infamous chick cliché. Mixing up *I love sex* with *I love you.*

Erin had known Sebastian Gallo now for two and a half days. If anything, she was a victim of sex at first sight. More than that would've been a true stretch of her credibility as a savvy, independent woman, assuming that's what she was. And she was. She knew she was. She just hadn't been terribly savvy about opening up her emotions to a man she only wanted to screw.

She should've kept her opening up to her girlfriends. But she knew Tess and Samantha had to be rolling their eyes that she'd managed to botch things so quickly. And then there was Cali who had her own issues with Will and didn't need to be hit first thing this morning with a blow-by-blow of Erin's night.

Erin's morning would be going a lot better if she could understand why Sebastian had left her bed so suddenly. For the first time this week she'd felt as if they were on the verge of making love. No, she *had* been making love. And she had a feeling that was exactly what had driven Sebastian away.

Because he was right. If all they were doing was sleeping together, she didn't need to know more of who he was than the little bit she'd learned. And the very fact that she'd asked meant…what?

"Yes, Samantha. I know. I know. I'm in love with the sex, not with the man," she grumbled to herself while pulling up her accounting software. But for some untold reason, Erin didn't believe a single word she said.

She went back to close down her inbox, stopping when the subject line *Anniversary Party—Paddington's On Main* caught her eye. The sender's name wasn't familiar, doubling her curiosity.

She opened it up, read through, read through a second time while her heart pounded wildly in her throat. The note was from the publicist who represented Ryder Falco. *The* Ryder Falco, the bestselling horror novelist dogging Stephen King's heels.

Falco was to be in Houston the weekend of Halloween and his publicist understood she was hosting a good-versus-evil themed party. Would she be interested in having Falco sign advanced copies of his newest Raleigh Slater release, *The Demon Begs to Differ?* After all, was there a single pop culture figure to better embody good-versus-evil than Ryder Falco?

Erin rocked back in her chair, shoved all ten fingers into her hair. This was totally insane! Unbelievable and wholly unreal! The post-party results of implementing every single one of last night's *Save Paddington's* brainstorming ideas wouldn't have half the impact of a Ryder Falco signing.

But how? No one knew of the recent conflict with Crewe Courtland's pre-grand opening event but Cali and Will and Sebastian...

Of course! This was Sebastian's doing. Erin hadn't a single doubt that this man about whom she knew next to nothing was responsible. Tied into his reticence to reveal personal information and the incredible library of books he owned, this made perfect sense. The business associates he'd mentioned had to be in publishing.

Surely he'd realize she'd put two and two together? Had he planned to tell her about making this amazing contact on her behalf? The very fact that he had made it...

She rocked her chair forward again, propped elbows on her desk, chin in her hands and stared at her electronic salvation. How would she ever be able to thank Sebastian for the invaluable gift when the very fact that he'd given it had her struggling for words?

HALLOWEEN NIGHT ARRIVED, finally, only to find Erin pacing madly through the bar, checking on the caterer's serving tables and fretting over decorations. The black and white, good-versus-evil theme had been played out from glittering snowflakes falling through shadowy spiderwebs to the jailhouse black and whites worn by the caterer's staff to the incredible array of visually contrasted food and drink.

Never in a million years would she have believed in the neutral color scheme's sensory appeal. But she had to admit the bar had never looked better. Even the black and white cookies worked, she realized, thinking about scarfing down a quick dozen. Nerves had kept her from eating for days and she suddenly found herself famished.

Yes, all the work she'd poured into the party had paid off—at least in presentation. She wouldn't change a thing. And her ace in the hole, Ryder Falco, virtually guaranteed she'd pull in the crowd she needed. She laughed, amused by the ridiculous understatement.

Ryder Falco guaranteed more of a crowd than she could ever fit into Paddington's and remain within code. Which was why she'd put two bouncers at the front door to man the line of Falco fans here for the autographing only. She realized she was dealing with a logistical nightmare and prayed for cool tempers and a zero percent chance of rain.

Once the bar hit capacity and hopefully stayed that way, the success of the night would be out of her hands and solely contingent on the work that had gone before. All she could do would be to cross her fingers that the party paid off at the cash bar and in returning customers.

She'd been a total wreck for the past three weeks, working to pull everything together and thinking this night would never arrive. The anniversary had loomed like an execution date when it should've been an exciting celebration marking the past year of her dedication on top of the dozens of years Rory had spent behind the bar. She hated that she still felt so bound to Paddington's instead of reveling in her success.

She and Sebastian had continued to see each other, their affair losing none of the initial intensity, settling into an intimately comfortable accord. She'd been grateful beyond reason for their shared schedule. More than once she'd stepped into her building's elevator at 3:00 a.m. and pushed ''7'', not bothering to stop on her floor before heading for his.

He was always awake as she'd known he would be. And he was always waiting, never surprised that she'd been drawn to his door. What had surprised her, however, was the way she'd so quickly grown secure enough in their involvement to invite herself into his shower instead of cleaning up in her own.

Sebastian's shower did come with one benefit hers didn't offer. Sebastian. She'd come to think of him as Poseidon, king of his water-filled domain. And, yes. Serving at Sebastian's feet had become one of her life's greatest pleasures—even if they'd yet to have sex in his bed. They'd slept there together but, the mornings she'd come awake in his place, she'd hurriedly dressed and left.

She'd never forgotten his first hasty flight from her bedroom almost a month ago. He'd never explained; she'd never asked. But she hadn't again made the mistake of thinking their coming together was about making love. They were here for the beauty of joined bodies. Love was the antithesis of having a Man To Do.

Her Man To Do had dodged her inquiries into his connection to Ryder Falco and the Halloween night signing, admitting to nothing more than calling in a few favors. After that, she hadn't asked him anything else personal. He seemed to prefer to talk about her, or to not talk at all.

She wouldn't be surprised to learn she was the first person he'd ever told about his showers. Or about the little toy truck, the ashes of burned-out fires, and a five-year-old's crushed birthday cupcake. And an intuitive female part of her doubted her knowing those crucial parts of his past sat well with the way he now lived his life.

More than once on the nights she did go straight home, she arrived to find him sitting outside her front door, waiting, wordlessly watching as she walked down the hall. Her heart blipped each and every time, and it was all she could do to rein in her emotions before she reached him. Harder still was the struggle to keep her feelings hermetically sealed while he stripped off her clothes and covered her with his bare body.

Tonight her emotions clashed in a virtual riot of ups and downs, sky highs and barrel bottoms. When deciding on her costume earlier in the month, she'd wavered between good and bad, uncertain whether or not embracing the dark side would reflect negatively at all on her position as hostess and as Paddington's owner.

Next she'd considered coming as the opposite of Sebastian, except that he'd never mentioned a costume or even his intent to attend. She'd tried not to be hurt, though it was difficult to maintain the detachment when she had started thinking of them as a couple of sorts.

Once this party was put to bed, she'd make the decision she knew she had to make about continuing their arrangement of seeking out one another for sex. Yes, it had been her idea to pursue Sebastian as a Man To Do, but it was also her female prerogative to change her mind. Continuing to deny her emotions was bound to blow up in her face. She loved him. Not that it did her a bit of good…

In the end she'd decided to dress as the epitome of good and had donned flowing white scarves over a cat suit of ecru-hued lace and presented herself as the mythical virgin sacrifice Cali had once accused Sebastian of looking ready to consume. Totally apropos, Erin thought, since he consumed her on a regular basis.

The setup for the Ryder Falco signing was absolutely perfect. Erin had paid the caterer extra to work with Falco's publicist and create an ambience suited to both the party theme and the author's notoriety as a mysterious recluse. She'd read his first novel, *The Demon Inside,* and had decided she'd stick with Nora Roberts for her fiction.

Falco's work was too sinister for Erin's tastes—exactly the reason the grotto of stones and live plants in the bar's darkest corner, lit with black lights casting a red-tinted ultraviolet glow, fit so well with the ambience of both the room and the man's reputation.

She circled through the room one more time then headed to her office to dress. When she returned thirty minutes later, Cali was already behind the bar, checking the crates of mugs and racks of wineglasses as well as the stock of hard liquor. She looked up as Erin joined her, twirling in a pirouette that sent her scarves floating.

Cali's eyes grew extra wide. "Oh, my God! You look totally awesome. Sebastian is so going to jump your bones."

Ignoring Cali's prediction, Erin raked her gaze over the other woman's costume of white shorts and a ribbed white tank that showed off her gorgeous curves. Cali also wore a halo atop of her mop of blond curls and a huge set of iridescent angels wings flapped on her back.

"You look pretty damn cute yourself." Erin felt her mouth twist into a wry grin. "Are you the angel of Will's salvation?"

"Something like that," Cali said with a bit of a prurient expression. "I couldn't decide on being good or bad and finally went for a combo."

Erin gave her friend another once over. "Well, you succeeded in a big way. He's not going to know what hit him."

Cali's smile begin to fade. "If he even notices."

"Why wouldn't he? How could he not notice?" Erin glanced toward the door as a party of four vampires came in.

"Oh, he'll notice, but he won't care." Cali pushed the crate of mugs back beneath the bar. "You know how guys get when they're pissed off. Whatever they're mad about is the only thing they can think of. They couldn't care less that someone went out of her way to make sure she looked good enough to eat."

"Wait a minute." Erin waved a scolding finger. "You know we're supposed to dress for ourselves, not for men."

"Puh-lease," Cali said with a huff. "What kind of *Cosmo* girl are you anyway? You can't tell me you dressed like that and never thought of Sebastian." A teasing light dawned in Cali's eyes. "Unless maybe you were thinking of seducing Ryder Falco."

Erin frowned and snorted. "Right. I dressed to seduce a man I don't even know."

"You didn't know Sebastian when you seduced him," Cali countered.

"That was different." Erin *had* known Sebastian.

She'd been making love to him for months in her mind. They just hadn't yet met—a horse of an entirely different color. "And I dressed this way for me. I don't even know if Sebastian is going to be here."

Cali's hands went to her hips. "What're you talking about? Why wouldn't he come?"

A trio of goth females—pale white complexions, dark lips and eyes, spiky black hair...oh, wait. One was a guy, Erin realized, shaking off the illusion. She turned back to Cali. "I imagine he will. He just never committed to coming."

"Maybe he assumed he didn't have to commit. Like he knew you knew he'd be here." Cali hesitated. "Y'all are still together, right? I mean, now I'm the one doing the assuming but you haven't said that y'all weren't still dating."

"C'mon, Cali. When have Sebastian and I ever *dated?* You know what our involvement is all about." It was exactly what it had been intended to be about from the get-go, Erin admitted, logic nicely stepping in to remind her of the facts.

"I know. I just thought..." Cali sighed, waved off the rest of her comment with one hand. "I don't know what I thought. I obviously have no business analyzing relationships since I don't even have a handle on my own."

"You never told me what's going on with Will. What's he being a grump about?"

"The screenplay. What else?" Cali picked up her serving tray to make a round through the bar. "He's not too happy that I discussed it with Sebastian."

"Hmm. Where is Will anyway?" Erin glanced up at the clock above the bar. "It's almost eight. Oh, God. It's almost eight." And Ryder Falco was due at nine.

"Can you tell me about Will later? I've got to make sure Robin knows Falco is her number one priority tonight."

"Relax, Erin. Robin's been working for you as long as I have. She knows her stuff. Everything'll be cool," Cali added before heading out into the crowd to circulate.

All Erin could do was take a deep breath and trust that Cali was right.

11

WALKING THROUGH Paddington's back door without first giving Erin full disclosure wasn't going to be fair. Sebastian knew that. Had for the last three weeks, in fact, recognized the building ache in his gut as guilt over what he was going to do. During tonight's short limo ride from his publicist's hotel to the bar, he sat expecting to physically implode.

Revealing his identity any earlier would've rendered the admission worthless. He knew that as well. Erin would've gone and canceled the signing and told him to get the hell out of her life. He'd be doing that soon enough. Tonight, as a matter of fact. But he didn't want to go without showing her that he'd never taken their involvement lightly.

He cared about her in ways he didn't know it was possible to care for another human being, ways he'd never once experienced throughout his thirty-four years. Except for the time spent learning what he had from Richie, Sebastian had been on his own from day one—and had followed his personal creed to the letter.

He never relied on anyone but himself. He never looked to another for what he couldn't beg, borrow or steal using his wits, his street smarts or the education he'd received in lockup, compliments of the State of Texas.

At least he'd never looked elsewhere before now.

Until lately, when he'd been looking to Erin for things he couldn't name, things indefinable yet significant, that had doubled his creative energy, spurred his enthusiasm toward the bitch of a project he'd been warily circling for months.

He didn't know what exactly was going on with her in regards to Paddington's and her grandfather. She hadn't been particularly up-front, had been damned evasive in fact, when he'd asked her those questions a few weeks ago while lying in bed at her side, holding her close, pulling her back into his body, content to do nothing but touch.

Okay, so he'd only been a temporary fix and not a permanent part of her life. She didn't owe him any answers. That said, he still wanted to know. His interest was real and true and drawn from that place where he felt too much and too strongly for this woman he was going to have to let go.

Slumped in the limo's back seat, he stared out the tinted window at the taillights on his left, shoving away the encroaching emotion he couldn't afford to feel. Not tonight. Tonight was going to be tough enough, worrying about her reaction to his deception, unable to talk to her, to explain until the signing's end.

Dealing with his own strange sense of loss on top was too much of a distraction to his focus. Later, maybe. After gaining the distance he needed. Then he'd be in a better position to look back objectively, to appreciate the time she'd allowed him into her life. For now, however, he would be the bastard he played so well.

Since Paddington's was spitting distance from his loft, his only caveat to the signing was going in costume. His publicist was used to his covert way of doing what little promotion he agreed to do and wasn't concerned by the subterfuge, just thrilled to have the reclusive Ryder Falco making a personal appearance.

Sebastian didn't want to be recognized in his own neighborhood after tonight. It might happen, but he was taking what precaution he could. Funny how tonight's chance for exposure registered lower on his personal radar than it had in the past. He added that inconsistency to his list of "laters" growing longer the more he sat and stewed.

The costume had worked. No one had looked at him twice on leaving his publicist's hotel where he'd dressed. Erin, of course, would recognize him immediately. Like he'd said, totally unfair. But it was either do it this way and give her the boost Paddington's needed, or never say a word about who he was and watch her suffer while Courtland's pulled in the landslide business that should've been hers.

He figured this way was the lesser of two evils. And, yeah. The signing went a long way toward assuaging a conscience he shouldn't have had. A self-reproach tied into the fact that he wouldn't be seeing Erin again after tonight. If he expected to string together one hundred thousand words that made sense and prove he had more in his creative repository than detectives and demons, he needed to shake off the sweetest distraction in which he'd ever indulged.

The mess he'd made with his newest Raleigh Slater story proved even recreational involvement with Erin was out of the question. She had too much impact on his state of mind when he needed complete clarity of thought. He couldn't afford the risk to his career. A career that was his entire life, his safety, sustenance and support.

His agent had been only marginally more tolerant of Sebastian's new project idea than had his editor. And understandably so. They both liked the guaranteed gravy of his Raleigh Slater series. Hell, he was partial to the stuff himself. His muse was another matter. She'd demanded he take up her gauntlet and give this new project his undivided attention—the very reason he had to cut himself off from Erin. From the little interaction he had with Cali and Will as well.

His success had come at a high price, but relying on self and self alone had taken him to the top. He hit the *New York Times* bestseller list with every new hardback release, and then again with the mass market printing a year or so later. He'd done it all on his own. And taking his career in a new and risky direction doubled the necessity of cutting off contact with the world outside the one in his mind.

He didn't expect Erin to understand. And the explanation he'd have to give her wouldn't satisfy her right to know or excuse his actions. But he had to do what he had to do without worrying about Erin being hurt.

He was having a hard enough time dealing with the strangling ache near his heart.

"OH MY GOD. OH MY GOD. Oh, Erin. Oh, God."

Erin hurriedly swiped the half-melted ice cube from the bar into her free hand and tossed both the ice and the rag into the bin beneath the bar. Ryder Falco. He was here. He was here. Oh, God. He was here. She sounded as hysterical as Cali.

She smoothed down her flowing scarves, a ridiculous effort that defeated the costume's entire purpose. "Do I look okay? First impressions are everything, you know." Cali worked so hard at swallowing, Erin worried her friend would choke. "Cali? What's wrong? Are you all right?"

Having scooted behind the bar and up to Erin's side, Cali grabbed Erin's upper arms and held tight. "Forget the first impressions. Just promise me one thing."

Erin frowned down at her friend's viselike hold. "Uh, Cali? Can this wait for a better time?"

Cali shook her head. "No. It can't. Now, promise me that, well, that…just promise me that you won't flip out or anything."

"Why would I flip out or anything?" Erin asked.

"Promise?" Cali's eyes both went wide. "I mean, this is important, Erin. This party is going to go a long way toward making sure you don't lose the bar. That's all that matters here, okay? You have to remember that."

Okay. This was getting weird. "What is it? The cops? The alcoholic beverage commission? Little green men?" When Cali didn't even crack a smile, Erin began to get nervous. She pried her arms free and said, "No flipping out. Or anything. I promise."

"If you do, I'm dragging you out of here. I swear." Cali made a spinning motion with one finger.

"No flipping out. I promise," Erin said then turned to face the grotto—and immediately forgot how to breathe.

Ryder Falco stood behind the grotto table, hands at his hips, the long tails of his black duster caught back like flared batwings. His black bad-guy hat was pulled low on his forehead; his black bad-guy bandanna was pulled high on the bridge of his nose. Only his eyes remained visible.

His eyes were all Erin needed to see to know who he really was. To remember the way he'd looked at her from across the bar the first night he'd come into Paddington's. To relive the moments he'd watched her only hours later as she'd walked into his home and shared his shower. Except suddenly his eyes seemed to be that of a stranger. She felt as if she didn't know him, had never known him, at all.

A man she assumed was his publicist stood at Sebastian's side, talking to the member of the caterer's staff responsible for the Falco book display. Yet, for all Sebastian's appearance of listening, Erin knew he wasn't. His attention was on her and no place else. They could easily have been the only two people in the room.

She loved a man who had lied to her, she realized, even as another painful truth struck. She had been equally dishonest with him—about the truth of her feelings, about the shallow and selfish reasons she'd invited him into her life. Still, her sin of omission hovered in the realm of petty. And, according to the weighted fist crushing her heart, Sebastian's ranked above the seven deadly.

And, now that she'd finally begun breathing again, she wanted to kill him almost as much as she wanted to do herself in. When had she become so blind? So gullible? And where could she get her hands on a weapon to slash his heart into shreds resembling hers? How in the hell did he plan to justify his deception? Anger quickly followed denial. This she could not wait to hear.

Erin took a deep breath and the first long step toward the grotto. Sebastian's gaze followed her the entire way. She kept her head up, her mouth set, her eyes focused straight ahead. Let him wonder. Let him squirm. She refused to give away an inkling of what she felt and held tightly to the power of that advantage.

Once she reached him, she pasted on a smile and extended her hand. "Mr. Falco? I'm Erin Thatcher. It's an honor to meet you. I owe you an amazing debt of gratitude and I'm not sure I'll ever be able to properly thank you."

Sebastian held on to her hand longer than required of a simple handshake. His eyes sparked and the bandanna barely muffled his voice. "No additional thanks are necessary, Ms. Thatcher. And the pleasure is all mine." Propriety finally demanded he release her. "This is my publicist, Calvin Shaw."

"Mr. Shaw. My thanks to you, as well." She shook the other man's hand, giving him her full attention while feeling Sebastian's devouring gaze. "I have no idea how you managed to convince Mr. Falco to leave his lair, but I'm incredibly glad that you did. You may have just saved the day."

Calvin Shaw crossed his arms over his chest and inclined his head toward Sebastian. "I'm the one glad to see Ryder here in the flesh. We get together so rarely that I've started to wonder if he's the fictional character instead of Raleigh Slater."

Erin forced an appreciative laugh when truly she felt like she might vomit. "Well, he looks like the real thing to me. Living, breathing. Totally three-dimensional. Not a work of fiction at all."

She returned her gaze to Sebastian, watched his eyes express all the things he was unable to say. She imagined the vein pulsing at his temple, the hard grinding tic in his jaw, the fullness of his lower lip pressed tight to his upper, all hidden behind his bandanna.

It was a small victory, but it was enough to know

he couldn't say a word without giving away the whole gig. "I hope you didn't have any trouble finding us. I know the construction has been terrible and we're not exactly one of the city's better known hot spots."

"No. No trouble at all," Calvin said, slapping a palm to Sebastian's back. "Ryder knew exactly where to find you."

"Really? That surprises me." She narrowed an eye in speculation. "Unless, of course, you've been here before. You should've introduced yourself. Your secret would've been safe with me."

"He claims the risk to his anonymity is too great. Or at least that's the excuse he gives me every time I try to book him a signing," Calvin said.

Erin was still waiting for Sebastian to answer. She wasn't leaving the grotto until he did, until he gave her a hint of an explanation for what felt like an unforgivable deception. If he thought she was putting him on the spot, all the better. Look what he was doing to her!

He pulled the brim of his hat even lower. "I have a couple of friends who live here in town. They love this place and wanted to help you out of your jam. Plus I knew it would get Cal off my back for a while."

"So a little bit of the goodness of your heart and a little bit of a peace offering?" Her grin grew brittle. "Your friends are lucky to have you. You've been extremely generous."

"I try to be. At least when it comes to the people I care about." He was good, way too good.

She wanted him to hurt like she did and resented his effortless cool. "Your friends are lucky to have you."

"I think I'm more lucky to have them." He offered a one-shouldered shrug—one almost apologetic, self-deprecating even. "Helps keep me sane in my isolation, knowing they're out there."

Erin fought back what felt too much like sympathy. He had done this to himself. She was not about to offer him her open arms. "Well, maybe now that you've seen how friendly we are, and that we're not out to devour hapless authors, you'll stop back by whenever you're in town."

Calvin rearranged a stack of books for maximum impact. "I'm hoping he'll see that getting out does not mean an automatic invasion of his privacy."

Sebastian might've smiled beneath the bandanna, but the emotion failed to reach his eyes. "Cal makes it sound like I never leave home."

"Do you?" she asked, willing Calvin to walk away and leave her to get the answers she wasn't getting.

"Sure," Sebastian said. "I walk through my neighborhood a lot. There's a great bar I frequent. Under the right circumstances, I can be downright sociable."

"Don't let him fool you." The table arrangement to his liking, Calvin pulled out Sebastian's chair. "He can be downright intimidating."

"Let's see." Erin gave Sebastian—The Scary Guy—a once-over. "Big guy. Head-to-toe black. Menacing eyes. Hmm. It's not hard to imagine that he might cause a ripple of fear." What *was* hard was standing here making small talk with a celebrity who had buried himself in her body as fully and completely as Sebastian had.

She supposed she should be starstruck. She wasn't. She was angry and hurt and beginning to shake from the emotional rush. She didn't know how she'd managed to pull off her role of hostess this long. She needed to get out of here—and now.

"Let me get you gentlemen a drink and then your fans can have at you. Again, thank you and enjoy the evening." She turned without waiting for Sebastian to respond and she never once looked back.

"DID YOU KNOW ABOUT THIS? That Sebastian was… that Sebastian *is* Ryder Falco?" Wearing black cape, mask, and gaucho-style Zorro hat, Will stood with a serving tray rather than a sword tucked beneath his arm, his gaze following the ebb and flow of the crowd while he questioned Cali.

She might've been more inclined to answer had he been talking to her and not to the room. Yes, he was busy doing his job. No, he was not ignoring her. But the last few weeks had been rather tense, what with their screenplay issues, and she found herself reading too much into everything he said. And everything he didn't say.

Especially when what he said had no basis. Like now. "Why would you think I would be privy to something even Erin didn't know?"

This time he did look at her, casting her a sideways glance from beneath his black mask, a glance that was just this side of a smirk. "Oh, I don't know. Something to do with the way *you* wanted *his* input on *our* screenplay? No, wait. How about the way you *went* to him for his input? Even though you knew I didn't give a damn what he thought?"

The heat of anger rose in a flush. Why was Will so intent on ruining her night? He knew every reason for what she had done. Knew, as well, the validity of the arguments she had made for the changes. He was just being a hardheaded egotistical man. And she wasn't sure she possessed the patience to put up with his crap no matter how she felt.

"Yes. I asked him, okay?" She stopped, took a calming breath, knowing she shouldn't have made the changes without telling Will.

But she'd wanted him to see the alterations once they were done—not while the story structure was in a state of flux. "I had no idea who he was when I did but, now that I know? His insights make a ton of sense. He was so intuitive about what would make the idea work."

Will went back to checking out the crowd, turning more than a cold shoulder Cali's way. "The changes you made might be your idea of what it needed but they sure weren't mine. I thought and I still think that it worked just fine as it was."

"You haven't even given it a chance. You haven't even read the story through since I tweaked it. You've just nitpicked certain scenes. That's hardly fair." Cali had known that having Sebastian look over the screenplay wasn't going to sit well with Will once he found out.

But she'd really wanted an outside opinion, one that would confirm her instincts if possible—exactly what Sebastian's input had done. She'd since gone through and made small and subtle changes where possible, keeping intact what she could of Will's skeleton. No matter that his feelings were hurt, she knew the story was stronger.

Now if she could only get him to agree. Then get him to understand why his major plot point wasn't going to work. But when he bodily turned to face her, banged his tray on the bar top and pulled off his mask, she didn't think much about his mood was agreeable.

"Me not reading the changes isn't fair but you making them without telling me is?" Without the obstruction of his glasses, Will's eyes glittered with sparks the likes of which Cali had never seen—

—and wasn't sure she found the least bit attractive. Her heart pounded painfully. "Please read it, Will. That's all I'm asking."

"I'm not sure I want to read it. Or work on it." His expression closed down. "It's not the story I wanted to tell anymore."

Cali wanted to stomp her foot in frustration, but she'd sworn tonight to be on her best angelic behavior for Erin's sake, and because she'd never make her point with Will by throwing a childish hissy.

"I did what I felt had to do, Will. I'm sorry you don't trust my motives or my instincts." Probably not a fair response but she'd be damned before she backed down on this—even though she had no idea how to correct the inevitable outcome of their current collision course.

The decibel level of the party crowd and party music rose higher, giving Will the option of shouting or of moving closer to be heard. He moved closer, offering Cali so many intimate reminders of having him near. The fight between her heart and her head and her warm and willing body grew fierce.

Will's expression grew fiercer. "And what exactly are your motives, Cali? To have it your way? To prove my way wrong by bringing in a celebrity author to vet your ideas?"

Pulling her gaze from Will's, Cali swept empty mugs into a dirty dish tub with no respect for their fragility. "You know I had no idea who Sebastian was until tonight. Erin didn't even know. She picked him to do because of their mutual attraction, not because of any fame and fortune.''

Will shook his head as if trying to settle a thought that didn't sit well. Or dodge a buzzing mosquito. ''Wait a minute. What do you mean, Erin picked Sebastian *to do?*''

Uh-oh. *Way to open mouth, insert foot.* The dish tub went under the counter. Cali got busy wiping condensation from the bar with the first rag she found, wishing she could wipe away the past few minutes of speaking without first gathering her thoughts. *Oh, why the hell not.* Honesty never killed a girl.

She shrugged out of her angel wings and shoved them beneath the bar. ''Erin went after what she wanted. An involvement with a man she found attractive. The very same thing men do all the time with women.''

She waited for a male denial, ready to go to the mat on this one, but Will kept his mouth shut, damn it, when she was finally itching for a fight. So she tried again. ''What Erin did was nothing but reversing a centuries-old dating practice. A woman picking up a man. Being gutsy enough to go against convention.''

''Man the torpedoes, full steam ahead?''

''Exactly.'' *And so there!*

Will took a minute to consider his reply, then came back with, ''Is that the same reason you came home with me?''

''What're you talking about?'' Cali asked, recognizing that she was about to be in really big trouble. ''I've come home with you more than a few times this semester.''

Leaving his tray on the counter, Will walked around behind, leaning an elbow onto the bar and forcing himself into Cali's personal space. His voice dropped to a volume meant only for her ears. "But you haven't come into my bed until recently. Kinda convenient that we started sleeping together about the same time Erin was doing Sebastian."

"I'm not sure I know what you're implying," Cali went back to wiping the bar. "Or even that I want to know."

"I'd think it's pretty obvious in context, Cali. Picking out a man you want to do? But, then again. It doesn't really matter, does it?" He spun his hat Frisbee-style down the bar and shrugged off his cape to go.

Cali grabbed at his elbow before he'd gotten completely out of her reach. "It matters to me. And, okay. I'll admit it. Yes, knowing Erin's plans did impact my decision to come home with you. But I'd wanted to come home with you for a very long time. I borrowed what I could of her guts and did it. I guess I shouldn't have."

The crowed milled noisily in the background while the world become nothing but the two of them and the tension of lovers at odds. Will stood still, the overhead track lighting casting over his hair a nimbus of light that was brighter than the one Cali wore. "If you wanted to be with me, Cali, it should've been about you and me. Not about what Erin decided to do."

He sounded too rational, too right. So much so that doubts burst rather than blossomed from recently sown seeds. "Does it really matter how we got together?"

"Does the end justify the means? Is that what you're asking?" He didn't give her time to say anything else before adding, "I think it does, yeah. Sex shouldn't be about a bet or a dare. And it sure shouldn't be some sort of twisted group seduction project.''

Cali balled her fist around the rag she still held, afraid Will was about to wash his hands of her. ''I can't believe you're being this way about the reason why I finally decided to come home with you. Or because of a lousy class project.''

Will's brows went up. ''Lousy? So now the screenplay is lousy?''

Cali pulled off her halo and flung it into the trash. ''No, it's not lousy. I wish you'd quit mucking up everything I say.''

Will shook his head, gave a laugh that was more about frustration and disbelief than about anything he might've found humorous. ''I'll tell you what's mucked up. That's the way you can take Sebastian's word about making changes without talking to me first. That you don't have that much respect for me. Or that much faith that I might eventually 'get it' if you drum it into my head often enough.

''I really might, you know.'' He paused then, studying her face with eyes that reflected a sad disappointment. ''But you didn't give me that chance. You went to Sebastian because he immediately told you what you wanted to hear. And, yeah. That is totally mucked up.''

He reached back and pulled out the copy of Sebastian's book he'd tucked into his waistband. He tossed the hardback volume onto the bar where it skidded to a hard stop against Cali's forearm. By the time she'd found a steady enough hand to pick up the book from the counter, Will had disappeared.

She opened the cover and read the inscription. Then she turned her back to the room and cried, while the words glared up at her. *It's a rare woman who is able to let a man be a man. You, Cali Tippen, are one of the best. I know it. And Will knows it, too. Friends always, Sebastian.*

ERIN COLLAPSED INTO THE gold velvet chair in her office because her desk chair wasn't big enough to contain her crushing despair. If despair was even the right word for the cloying fog that had wound itself in and around the flowing scarves of her costume until her feet felt too heavy to lift, her body too sluggish to move.

Her heart too brutally battered to ever beat again.

Ridiculous, really. So what if Sebastian hadn't breathed a word about his alter ego? They'd never agreed to any sort of full disclosure. What they were doing here was all about sex. He'd found an easy lay. She'd tumbled him as a lark. No one said their involvement meant anything more.

But it did. For both of them. Because, no matter what bullshit he'd given her weeks ago about calling in favors, there was absolutely no reason for him to have revealed his identity to save Paddington's. Not unless he had feelings for her. He could've had any woman he wanted. But he'd wanted her.

And she knew she'd fallen in love with him that first night in his shower.

After welcoming Sebastian and his publicist and feigning excitement when her giddiness had been more about hysterical misery, she'd spent the last two hours avoiding the grotto and circulating through the crowd as befitting her position as hostess. She'd laughed and refilled drinks and flirted and danced when hijacked onto the dance floor—until she couldn't fake the light-hearted charade any longer.

She'd had to get away. And now she sat rubbing at the headache building behind the bridge of her nose.

God, she needed to talk to Cali. But Cali was busy running the show Erin should've been out there handling. She wasn't about to add to her best friend's stress load, so she pushed up from the comfy velvet chair and dropped into the one in front of her keyboard instead.

From: Erin Thatcher
Sent: Saturday
To: Samantha Tyler; Tess Norton
Subject: The Secrets That Men Keep

Y'all were wondering if the things Sebastian told me were true? The secretive things I hinted at earlier? Well, they are. And it's worse—or better—depending on your viewpoint.

I'm sleeping with Ryder Falco. No, I'm not kidding. Ryder Falco is my Man To Do. I guess that wouldn't be so bad if I hadn't fallen in love…

Erin,
who can't even think of anything else to say

She hit Send and collapsed back in her chair. Not only couldn't she put together another cognizant sentence, she also couldn't get beyond the dimensions of the sacrifice Sebastian had made. For her. What he'd done said so much about the man he was. And that, more than anything, made loving him impossible.

Already she suffered enormous guilt at the thought of letting down the grandfather whom she'd dearly adored. Now she had Sebastian's sacrifice to come to grips with. And then there was all the work Cali had done. And Will. Not just in the bar and cohosting the party, but in their amazing concern and effort to bail her out of the Courtland's debacle.

And the worst part was that, after all of this, ungrateful cow that she was, she wasn't even sure she wanted to save Paddington's.

Before she could flagellate herself further, or wrap one of her flowing scarves around her neck and pull it tight, the e-mail chime sounded. Good grief. What were either of her cyber-girlfriends doing up at this ungodly hour?

From: Samantha Tyler
Sent: Saturday
To: Erin Thatcher; Tess Norton
Subject: Re: The Secrets That Men Keep

Erin! I don't know which is freakier, that this guy turns out to be a mega-celebrity or that you are in love with him!

But I sure as hell want to hear more. There's a whole, whole lot you're not telling us. Judging by the tone of your e-mail, I'd say you aren't overjoyed either about who he is or the fact that you're in love with him. Or maybe you're just exhausted and overwhelmed? I hope that's all it is.

In any case, you owe us one whole cartload of details, so give! I won't rest easy until I hear.

Wondering and worrying and crossing my fingers hard that it works out for you, honey.

Samantha

Too bad there wasn't going to be anything to work out, Erin mused, closing out the e-mail. Samantha couldn't know that, of course. Couldn't know that Erin had managed to screw up the life of the man she loved.

12

SEBASTIAN KNEW HE'D FIND Erin in the office.

He'd seen her disappear behind the safety of the door an hour ago, but he'd been stuck in the shadows of the grotto, developing carpal tunnel from repeatedly signing his name. His own fault, he reminded himself, scratching out *Ryder Falco* another fifty times.

He wasn't worried that she'd been in there all this time falling apart. She was too strong to let that happen. She had no reason to let that happen. During their time together, he'd been more than careful to make sure he did nothing to encourage her emotional involvement. Not that he'd succeeded. He'd seen too much hope, too much longing in her eyes.

Unless what he'd seen was his own damn reflection—a highly likely possibility.

Never had he been so close to abandoning every principle by which he'd lived since he'd taken back his life. And all because of what Erin Thatcher made him feel about her—and about himself. The hope was the worst, the sense that she'd be there any time he extended his hand when he knew better than to reach out in the first place. Yeah, the hope was the main reason he wouldn't be seeing her after tonight. If he ever finished up this damn signing…

Ninety minutes later, he'd depleted the books supplied by the distributor and finished with the fans who'd brought copies of their own. As Ryder Falco, he escaped through the back door, climbing into his publicist's limo rather than taking the chance of being followed on foot. Three blocks later he was out of his costume and demanding the driver pull over.

Wearing biker boots and jeans and the black T-shirt he'd had on beneath his Aztec print western shirt and long black duster, and having ditched both the bandanna and broad-brimmed black Stetson, he headed back to Paddington's and, as Sebastian Gallo, walked in through the open front door.

He ignored the lingering party-goers, ignored servers clearing tables, ignored the caterer's crew dismantling the grotto, pulling down spiderwebs and snowflakes, even ignored Cali Tippen as she tried to flag him down. Unless he found Erin's office door locked, he wasn't stopping for anyone.

He didn't stop, in fact, until he'd shut the door behind him. This time he made sure to turn the lock. He had too many things to say and no patience to deal with interruptions. Erin sat at her desk, her head down on crossed arms, those sheer scarves draped over her body that drove him wild. A fall of red hair covered her face. He steeled himself as she raised her head.

At least she hadn't been crying. That much he was desperately glad to see. It was the blanch of white skin, however, and the purple boxerlike bruises underneath her eyes that told him discovering his identity had not been one of the better moments of her life. She was beaten up and badly so.

"Why didn't you tell me?" she asked, her voice a steady whisper, her brows drawn together in a frown of frustrated confusion and loss.

The loss is what got to him the most when it

should've made what he had to do that much easier. He wasn't always big on honesty being the best policy, but tonight he owed her no less. And he'd get there. Eventually. "I never tell anyone."

"You told half of Houston tonight," she accused.

"Not really." He moved away from the door and sank into the cushy crushed velvet chair opposite her desk. "Thanks for accommodating me the way you did. The cave was great."

"It was a grotto."

"It was perfect," he repeated.

She sat up straighter, straight enough to lean back in her chair, brace her elbows on the chair arms and protectively lace her hands over her midsection. "Well, your publicist did say you weren't much for exposure. I mentioned that I'd heard that. Had I known we shared experience with one and the same person, I could've given him my personal insight."

Sebastian shrugged, though none of what he felt registered on the scale labeled nonchalance. "Like I said, I don't tell anyone. Ever."

She met his gaze directly, her eyes taking on a life that hadn't been there when he'd first walked into the room. And a fiery life at that. "Why *did* you tell me?"

"It was time." That was honest enough. "I could hardly pull off the signing without you knowing who I was." Another bite of indisputable truth.

"That's what I mean." She put her chair into a side-to-side swivel. "Why would you go to so much trouble to keep your identity secret and then blow it like that? Paddington's is such small potatoes in the scheme of your career."

"You're not small potatoes." And that was as honest as it got. Nothing else he said would ring with a louder sincerity.

"Compared to Ryder Falco?" She swiveled faster, color returning to her cheeks. "Oh, I think that I am."

"We're not talking about what you think."

"That's patently obvious. If I had known what you were going to do…" Bringing her chair to a complete stop, she shook her head and let the sentence trail, though they both knew what she was thinking.

Frankly, he hadn't expected her to so easily make his argument for him. "And that's exactly the reason I didn't tell you before."

"I suppose I should be grateful that you've come to explain it to me now, after the fact, instead of disappearing out into the night." She huffed. "It all makes sense now. The walking, the thinking, the steaming the wrinkles out of your brain."

One ankle squared over the opposite knee, Sebastian slumped down to sit on his tailbone, shoved both hands back over his hair and laced his fingers there on top of his head. "I've never lied to you, Erin. You know that. I was vague. Ambiguous. Elusive, even. But I never said a word that wasn't the truth."

She crossed one long leg over the other. Filmy scarves fluttered with the movement then settled to expose thighs near enough to nude to toss a blip into the rhythm of his pulse. Her chin jutted forward—her spirited nature warning him he wasn't in for an easy time of it.

"Then what the hell is this truth?" she asked. "You get to call all the shots in this arrangement, is that it? I don't have any say in how we play things out?"

"This was my shot to call, Erin."

"No. It wasn't. Not when you did it because of—"

"Because of you?" he asked, cutting her off as frustration mounted. "Why else would I do it?"

"I don't know, Sebastian." The skin over the knuckles of her laced fingers tightened. "I'm too tired to deal with this cryptic conversation. Why don't you just tell me why and save me the trouble of sorting out the puzzle pieces?"

She was neither dense nor naive. What she was was wracked with some misplaced guilt over a decision *he* had made. A telling realization that he knew her that well, when he'd worked hard to convince himself none of his knowledge about her went that deep.

"I've watched you drive yourself insane the past few weeks, working to pull this party together. And then Courtland's comes along with an advertising budget you don't have and, what?" He dropped his hands to the chair arms and held tight. "You expect me to sit back and let you be steamrolled when I can stop it from happening? I don't think so."

"Allow me to be skeptical about your altruism. For whatever reason, you've made it a point to avoid involvement with the city, with your fans, even with your neighbors," she said and waved an encompassing hand. "Except for me. And I really don't buy that you'd break your long time seclusion for the sake of good sex."

Sebastian ground his jaw. "I didn't do it because of the sex."

"Then that leaves you doing it because you feel you owe me for something, which you don't." Her spine straightened further. "You haven't taken advantage of me. You haven't demanded anything I haven't wanted to give. And this is not the sort of sacrifice one lover makes for another…not when being lovers has nothing to do with being in love.''

His jaw remained tight, making it hard to maintain a level tone of voice. "Can you find a place for friendship in your conspiracy theory?''

She considered his explanation for no longer than it took her to blink it away. "This seems to go beyond the bounds of friendship.''

Talk about hardheaded women. "Wouldn't you do the same for Cali?''

"Sure, but Cali and I have been best friends for three years. You and I have been intimately acquainted for only a month. I just can't make the same leap. It's way too much of a sacrifice.'' She pressed her lips together as if holding back the rest of what she had to say. And then she let it go. "I can't decide which is stronger. The need to thank you, or the urge to tell you to take a flying leap.''

Sebastian's irritation began a slow upward climb, approaching that place where he was afraid he was going to regret his words—and very possibly his actions. "Why are we even having this conversation, Erin? What's done is done. It can't be changed. All we can do is go on from here.''

Erin tossed up both hands. "Sure. Let's go on from here. Where exactly are we going to go?''

Take it slow, bonehead. Nice and slow and easy. If he could manage to find the right words—and how hard could that be for a writer—they might emerge from tonight with at least their friendship intact. "Your party was a hit so, if anything, I'd say you're headed into your second year of business in a very big way.''

For an extended heartbeat she maintained eye contact, allowing him to see the flurry of thoughts as her mind processed the implication of his suggestion. But the longer he watched, the longer she remained silent, the clearer it became that a second year of business failed to offer any appeal.

He shifted in the chair and leaned forward, bracing both forearms on his side of her desk. "I don't get it, Erin. Isn't this what you wanted?"

She raised a questioning brow. "Which part? Yes, I wanted the party to succeed. I can't stand the idea of blowing all that effort. Or all that money."

She might as well have added the "but" because Sebastian heard it loud and clear. "And the second year of business? After the amazing first year you just celebrated?"

Again she paused, taking a long moment to reflect before asking, "Was it really that amazing?"

Was she looking for validation? Surely she recognized the height of her success. "Your granddad would've loved what you've done."

"You think so?" she asked, a tiny quirk lifting one corner of her mouth. She pushed up from her chair, crossed to the corner file cabinet above which hung an eight-by-ten photo of Rory behind the bar of the original Devon Paddington's.

She stared at the framed snapshot, then turned to lean against the file cabinet, her hands behind her and the scarves of her costume floating like ethereal ghosts in the air. "I'm not so sure I agree."

"Why wouldn't he?" he asked, then quickly changed his approach. "Don't forget. I've lived here awhile. I've watched what you've done from the beginning."

She was too far away. Sebastian rose, walked to the end of her desk and propped a hip on the corner. "In one year you've turned this place from beer hall to a slick urban bar.''

She gave a delicate little snort, stared down at the toes of her clear glass-looking shoes. "And now I'm bringing in authors. Next thing I'll be having poetry readings and performance art and who the hell knows what else."

"And what's wrong with that?"

She rolled her eyes, dropped her head back against the wooden drawers. "Only that Rory is probably turning over in his grave."

Amazing. Totally frigging amazing. "You know, Erin. You've just had a kick-ass party. The crowd was capacity all night. Yes, I know. A lot of them came when they heard about the signing."

Erin huffed. "A lot? Try seventy-five percent."

"That's bullshit and you know it. They came for me, but they stayed for you. Because of what you've accomplished here with what your granddad left you." He crossed his arms over his chest so he wouldn't choke her into admitting the error of her ways. "And you can't even enjoy your own success because you're worried what Rory might think."

The fire returned to her eyes; her chin came up higher, her shoulders straighter than before. "Rory gave up everything, Sebastian. Everything. He came here to take care of me when I was eleven years old. He never had a life of his own except for this place. So, yeah. Forgive me if I'm a little bit concerned that I'm not taking care of it the way he'd want."

How could this same woman who'd been unbelievably intuitive in her dealings with him not be equally perceptive about the man who'd raised her? "Your granddad loved being his own boss. The independence made him incredibly happy. Here or in Devon, it didn't matter. And you know that, the same way you know he'd want the same for you.''

For the first time since he'd known her, tears shimmered in her eyes. Her lower lip quivered and her entire presence grew vulnerable and small. He couldn't stand the distance between them any longer.

He went to her, pulled her into his arms, pressed her cheek to his chest, his chin to the top of her head and inhaled the fragrance of her hair that reminded him of green fields and sunshine.

He was so far gone he wondered how he'd survive walking away. "Be true to yourself. That's the best way to honor his memory."

"What if being true to myself means dumping the bar?"

"The only way you can disappoint anyone is by not doing what's right for you. Even if it means selling the bar." Her hands slipped around his waist, making it harder to ready himself to back away. "We all have to do what's right for us. That's the only thing that matters in the end."

For a moment it seemed like she'd forgotten to breathe and then she stiffened and asked, "And what's right for you?"

You can do this. You can let her down easy. Yeah, he could let her go and drop his heart in the trash can on his way out the door. "A book I've wanted to write for a while. It's different, not my usual Slater stuff. First I had to convince my agent I wasn't going to crash his gravy train. Then I had to work out a schedule with my demon contracts."

He gave a small shrug before stepping away. "Basically, the time had to be right."

Erin threaded fingers through her hair, pushing it out of her face. She stepped around him and moved to the far side of her visitor's chair, as if needing both the barrier and the distance. "So, now the time is right?"

He nodded, and he followed, even though he knew what he had to say would be best said with the cushion of space she'd given him instead of from where her subtle scent enticed him. "I haven't been this excited about a project in a very long time."

He wanted to add more, to tell her this last month spent in her company had renewed his creative energy. He wanted to explain how he'd fed off her enthusiasm for her party, off her drive to save a business she considered more burden than blessing.

He wanted her to know that with her, in her, he'd found the part of himself missing since he left to fend for himself at eleven years of age. And that he'd finally learned his soul had never been stronger than since finding its mate.

But those weren't the things to say when the truth was he didn't know any other way to live than on his own.

"That means you're leaving, doesn't it?"

"I'll still live above you."

"But you're leaving. You won't be around."

He nodded because she'd put into words the number one truth he couldn't bring himself to admit. "No. I won't."

And then he went to her, took her face in his hands, cradling her gently as he lowered his head and brushed his lips to hers. She was so incredibly sweet when she trembled. And she tasted like so many good things he hadn't yet had time to explore.

He moved his hands into her hair and pulled her

lower lip between his until she closed her eyes and shuddered, her hands moving to his back where she pulled his T-shirt free from his jeans and caressed the skin beneath.

She held him tenderly, telling him with tiny flicks of her tongue to his of her feelings. Of the wonder of what they'd found together. Of the regret bound in the impossibilities of their lives. He hated that he'd caused her to suffer and soothed what he could of her sorrow by ending the kiss to hold her close.

She sighed into his T-shirt, the warmth of her breath heating the fabric damp from her tears. When he finally set her away, he found it difficult to speak, difficult to swallow. So he squeezed her hand once, his fingers trailing over hers as he let her go and headed for the door.

ERIN DOUBTED THERE would be another Halloween night in history to rival the gore of this one. She couldn't think about Sebastian or Paddington's or anything right now. Right now, all she had the will to do was climb into her car and go home.

First she had to close up the office so she could close up the bar and the kitchen. She was definitely going to have to pay Cali double-time for taking care of things the last half hour. Yet, before Erin could make the short walk to shut down her computer, another e-mail arrived.

From: Tess Norton
Sent: Saturday
To: Erin Thatcher; Samantha Tyler
Subject: Re: The Secrets That Men Keep

Ryder EFFING Falco? You have got to be kidding. Oh, my God, you know how much I love his books. I've read every one. Some twice! Holy shit, girl!

Actually that expletive was more about that, uh, little bomb you dropped. Love? Did I read this correctly? LOVE as in LOVE?

My, my. Not exactly the goal of the Men To Do project, but then, who cares? You're in love. What you didn't mention is if he is in love back. How could he not be, but still. Men are a strange species, and I've found it's best if I don't try to anthropomorphize them. <g> Seriously, I need to hear the details about this, and I need to hear your voice, and I need to be much wiser than I am, which is going to be hard to do in the next 24 hours, so don't do anything drastic. Chocolate. My best (and seemingly only) advice. Love, Tess

Well, one thing was certain, thought Erin, shutting down her computer. Sebastian did not love her in return. He liked her well enough. He lusted after her without a doubt. His investment had to be more than physical or he would never have revealed his identity. But love? Ha! Love was not part of his emotional capacity.

Or, if it was, he refused himself the pleasure, burying his head in make-believe worlds where life was simply black and white. She wanted to hate him for it, but all she could think of was that little toy truck.

A knock on the door brought Erin's head around expecting Cali. But it was Robin, one of the other servers to work the party tonight. "Where's Cali?"

"Said she was feeling like crap. I told her to beat it

and I'd finish up. Which I have, so…'' She pulled off the tail of her cat-woman costume. ''I'm heading out. The caterer will be back Monday afternoon with a truck to pick up the fountain and rocks.''

''Thanks for handling the cleanup.'' Robin, Laurie, Cali and Will had all gone above and beyond the call of duty. ''I think the fact that we actually pulled this off wiped me out. I hadn't realized how exhausted I was.''

''You deserved the downtime. You just missed a hell of a party. Oh, there's a guy out here who's been waiting to talk to you. We told him you were busy but he insisted,'' Robin said, adding air apostrophes around the last word.

''I need to come out and lock up anyway.'' Erin crossed the room, cut off the light and locked the office door. She hoped her visitor was made of strong stuff because she had a swift kick ready for anyone with a penis. ''I'll show him out, if you'll hang around for a minute?''

''Not a problem.'' Cat tail now draped around her neck, Robin grabbed her purse from beneath the bar. ''He's at the front door. I'll leave that way.''

''Thanks, Robin. And for all your help tonight, too.''

''Sure. I'll wait here till you're done.'' She slid into the nearest booth while Erin headed toward the front door.

Her visitor leaned one shoulder on the brick wall and wore nothing remotely resembling a Halloween costume—unless his costume was the epitome of *dressed for success*.

His hair was fashionably short, grayed at the temples. He wore a long black wool coat over a pair of designer pants and Italian loafers worth more than her black and white cookie bill.

Intriguing, she thought, and approached. "May I help you?"

"Ms. Thatcher?" he asked and she nodded. "My name is Nolan Ford."

Erin took his offered hand and shook. A firm businesslike shake. "What can I do for you Mr. Ford?"

"I wonder if you've ever considered selling this place because I'd like very much to talk to you about buying it."

THANK GOODNESS FOR twenty-four hour Kinko's, Cali thought, ruining yet another page of the screenplay. She'd had the sense to make five sets at the copy center earlier, anticipating that she'd never get the changes reversed the first time out.

Having the disk would've made this whole groveling process easier. But her disk was in Will's laptop where she'd left it after making the initial revisions based on Sebastian's suggestions. She didn't have a computer of her own, using Will's or renting time at Kinko's.

Since she'd saved her edits over the original file without making a backup, it was six in one hand, a half dozen in the other whether she did this on the screen or by hand. She supposed Will might have a printed copy of the original since he was so emotionally attached to the beast. But knowing his version would never pass a credibility test, she'd tossed all the copies she'd had.

Yes, she'd learned her lesson. Always make a backup file. She'd learned another lesson as well. *Men sucked.* She wadded the paper and tossed the crumpled ball across the room. No, that wasn't exactly the truth.

Not all men sucked and men didn't suck all of the time. But right now neither scenario fit her mood.

Especially since she was rapidly compromising her own self-respect. She was giving in because she didn't want to lose the one man who meant more to her than any single man before. Her rationalization that this was only a project for a grade and not any sort of life-altering decision didn't do much to keep the situation from rubbing against her personal grain.

She was getting close to hating herself as much as she hated Will. Hating Will made perfect sense, after all, since she loved him so desperately. And this last week of working together and taking classes together hadn't gone particularly smoothly since they hadn't said a single civil word.

A knock on the door of her efficiency apartment sent her pencil scrabbling off the end of the page. *Finally.* Erin and the damn bottle of wine she'd promised to drop by with when she'd phoned earlier this afternoon. Cali tossed her paperwork to the love seat and hopped up to get the door.

Only it wasn't Erin. It was Will, looking like his Sunday off hadn't been very relaxing either. He hadn't shaved and his glasses didn't do much to hide the circles under his eyes. She supposed she didn't look much better. She was wearing ragged denim shorts and the stubble on her legs matched that on his face. She'd been sleeping alone this last week. Shaving had hardly seemed to matter.

Oh, well. She was human. If she hadn't been she wouldn't be tearing her heart out over what she had done and what she was now doing with the screenplay. She would've cared less about Will's feelings and more about the grade. Cared more as well about getting him to admit he was wrong. Suddenly, that didn't seem to matter.

Wearing a distressed leather bomber jacket and gray athletic T-shirt, he leaned against the doorjamb, shoulders shrugged up against the cold, hands stuffed in the pockets of his baggy black cords. "Hi."

It was all he said. Cali gave a little wave, an even smaller smile.

Will inclined his head. "Do you mind if I come in?"

She pulled the door farther open and ushered him inside. She still didn't trust her voice. She pushed the door closed and turned the lock out of habit—not because she planned to never let him go.

And then she remembered the screenplay. The pages tossed willy-nilly over the love seat. She remembered at the same time Will spied her work.

"What're you doing?" His gaze cut sharply back to hers.

She crossed her arms over her chest. Her faded pink sweatshirt hiked up to expose her middle. "Trying to fix a big mistake."

He dropped into the seat probably still warm from her body and picked up the pages, shuffling them into order, flipping through them one at a time. Cali could only cringe at her very raw, very rough, way too often sarcastically noted corrections.

And then there was that note on the fourth page...

Her face flamed and she jumped forward to snatch the pages from his hands. Too late, of course, because he held them high, reached out and pulled her into his lap.

She tumbled there like the biggest buffoon. Her heart on her sleeve wasn't even an issue. Not when it was right there in a sketch of Cupid shooting his arrow and a tree-carving caption that read C.T. + W.C. 4-EVER.

"Don't be so grabby," he said. "I want to see what you've done."

"I haven't done much," she said, hoping to dissuade him from looking beyond the first page or two. "I was trying to remember as much as I could of your original version."

"*My* original version, huh?" Will settled back to get comfortable, spreading his knees and shifting Cali into the corner of the love seat and onto one thigh, her legs draped across his lap.

He had one arm around her back so that she rested in the curve of his shoulder. His other hand was busy flipping through the pages. She wasn't sure whether she dreaded more his discovery of her leg stubble or her childish scrawl.

He got to the fourth page and stopped, glancing the length of the page before canting his head around to look her in the eye. "What happened to this being a joint project?"

"I think it's obvious that we've jointly gone about as far as we can go. We might share the same idea for the end, but we'll never agree on the means to get us there." She looked at him, and it was all she could do not to lean forward and nuzzle his cheek.

She knew his scent and his warmth and his texture and it was so hard not to wrap her arms around him. Especially with the way he was looking at her, with an expression she couldn't quite decipher but raised her hopes nonetheless. "Why did you come here, Will?"

His eyes grew glassy and bright. He heaved an enormous sigh as if blowing out the last of his pent-up anger. And then he grinned his Cheshire cat grin. "To tell you that you were right. That I was wrong. That I don't have half the talent you do and absolutely no confidence that I'll ever learn enough to 'get it.'"

"What are you talking about? Your instincts are great. And we all need a little fine-tuning now and again. I'm certainly not perfect. If I were, the changes would've been my idea, not Sebastian's." She stopped talking then, realizing she'd lifted her hand to cup his cheek and remembering nothing about deciding he needed her touch.

Her feelings for him were that natural, that right, and that awareness made it easy to make the admission she'd been holding back. "I only did it because I love you."

Will dropped the pages he was holding and reached up, covering her fingers where she still caressed his face. He squeezed, then moved her hand to his mouth and kissed her palm.

With his gaze locked on hers, he softly said, "Then love me by making me be my best."

Six Months Later...

GOODBYE, PADDINGTON'S. Hello, rest of my life.

Erin would never have believed she could walk away from the sale of the bar with such a light heart. Especially after the months of angst and worry over doing the right thing for herself and for Rory.

Now those days and nights seemed as if they'd never happened. She owed such a debt of gratitude to Cali and Will, to Tess and Samantha, and to Sebastian for making her face all the truths she needed to face.

She owed a debt of a different nature to Nolan Ford,

for his timely toss of a life preserver into the middle of her personal storm.

She and Sebastian had spoken a few times over the last several months but had never shared more than could be said in a six-floor elevator ride, a trek through the parking garage, or while standing and sorting mail in the basement mailroom.

His book was going well, he'd told her. Practically riting itself; he hoped to finish before summer. She was glad, she'd told him. Because that meant by summer they'd both be free of the pressing obligations wedged between their friendship.

He hadn't had much to say in response, but that was okay. Erin had learned how to hear what he didn't say by looking into his eyes. His eyes had given her hope. Every time they'd run into one another, his eyes had given her hope.

She'd sold the bar and gotten her act together. This fall she would be starting back to school to finish her degree, though in truth she'd be starting over. The study of business had never truly held any appeal. And after the publicity generated by the Paddington's On Main Halloween party, she was much more interested in marketing.

But right now it was summer.

She didn't know if Sebastian had finished his book, but he hadn't turned her away when she'd called earlier and told him she was on her way up. She took that as a good sign that he wasn't averse to seeing her. She never had really thought he'd be averse. She just wasn't sure how welcoming he might be.

She couldn't let doubts of his reaction deter her. This is what she had to do. The same way she'd sold Paddington's and, working with her advisor, put together a plan to return to school.

It had taken her a while to come to grips with the truth of what Sebastian had said that night he'd walked out of her life. But he had been right. Rory had given her the means to pursue her dream. He'd loved her and would never have wanted her to run the bar unless it meant as much to her as it had always meant to him. What she'd been doing, she'd been doing for Rory out of a misplaced sense of guilt and obligation.

And she'd finally looked beyond the tangible assets of Rory's gift to the intent. The same way she'd finally come to accept the intent behind Sebastian's sacrifice. And that was the reason she was here. His exposure as Ryder Falco had not been about saving the bar, but about showing her the worth and the depth of a man's love.

A love she returned beyond reason.

She knocked; he didn't answer. She turned the knob, found the door open, let herself in. The front room was dark, blues playing on the stereo. She'd never been up on her artists but she was pretty damn sure this was B.B. King. He was singing "Hold On! I'm Comin'."

She wanted to laugh out loud at the fluke. Especially since she knew Sebastian would be in the shower listening to the music pour through the bathroom's speakers built into the ceiling above the steamy enclosure. She couldn't wait to join him.

She found him exactly where she'd known he would be. She'd opened the door to the bathroom to the sound of the blues and running water and Sebastian was there, sitting beneath the center showerhead, legs spread wide, his palms on his thighs, the whole of his sex heavy from the heat.

For a very long moment she could do nothing but stare.

He made such a picture of male beauty that breathing no longer seemed to matter as much as filling her senses with the memories of making love. And it had been love. Maybe not that very first time here in this shower. She hadn't even known him then. And still she didn't know all she wanted to know. What she hoped she'd have a lifetime to learn.

She slipped out of her clothes and stepped into his arms, knowing no decision she'd ever made had been so right. He felt glorious. All male and head-to-toe hard and slick and wet. She loved the bunch of muscles at his shoulders and running along either side of his spine.

She loved the strength in his neck, the tendons and veins there as well as those in his forearms. There wasn't a thing about him she didn't find perfectly gorgeous. *Especially that,* she thought, grinning as his erection came to life against her belly.

Lifting her head, she leaned back far enough to look into his eyes. His expression epitomized tenderness. And love. And the pain of a man caught in an unbearable loss. So silly. He'd never lost her. She'd always been here.

"Do you remember when you kissed me Halloween night in my office?" He nodded and she continued. "I couldn't tell you then that I love you. So I'm telling you now."

"I love you, too." And his mouth came down hard to take possession of hers. His lips devoured, his tongue swept over hers like a tidal wave from which she had no way to escape.

As if escape was any more of an option than telling him no when he backed her into the wall and urged her legs around his waist. He pressed forward, upward, filling her body with one smooth thrust, then another, another, another still until he'd set a rhythm from which there was no return.

His mouth never left hers, not for a second, not even when he came and took her with him, tumbling her into an incredible abyss and catching her when she reached the end of her completion.

Only then, when she'd finished, when he'd seen to the last of her tremors, grinding there where she needed the friction one last shuddering time, only then did he lower her to her feet and relinquish possession of her mouth.

Thank goodness because she could hardly catch her breath by breathing through her nose. Water cascaded and she held him tight, feeling his heartbeat thunder beneath her cheek resting on his chest. She didn't think she'd ever in her life been this happy, this complete.

Or this amazingly tired. "Tell me a story."

He chuckled, stroked a hand down the back of her hair. "Once upon a time—"

"No." She shook her head, his skin sweetly salty when she stuck out her tongue and lapped. "Get to the good part."

This time when he spoke, he did so on a quivering comet tail of emotion. "And they lived happily ever after."

Epilogue

"Written with Ryder Falco's flair for suspense but with a new emotional pitch that is total Sebastian Gallo, *The Secrets of an Innocence* captures the journey of a man's life as it builds to a memorable climax. This is an amazing love story, at once heartbreaking and full of hope."

—Publisher's Monthly

THE SECRETS OF AN INNOCENCE
By Sebastian Gallo
Chapter One

It came to him later that the defining moment of his life had occurred when he wasn't even looking. The beauty of the memory caught him off guard as had the event at the time. He'd never imagined he'd need one single woman in his life more than he'd feel the need to breathe. But he had.

She'd been his sustenance for all the long years of his life, the safety net catching him at every fall, the support that kept him upright when the world around him came tumbling down. He loved her more than he'd ever known a man could love a woman. And, most amazing of all, she loved him back.

Don't miss the next blazing hot story in the
MEN TO DO *mini-series!*
Check out Jo Leigh's
A DASH OF TEMPTATION,
coming in January 2003 from BLAZE.

Prologue

To: Erin
CC: Samantha
From: TessThePlantLady@hotmail.com
Subject: Men I'm Not Going To Do

Okay, picture this: I'm with Brad. He's wearing Armani and he smells like cashmere on ice. His hair is perfect, including the obligatory rakish bangs across his forehead. His frown is fetching, his gaze hurt.

Me: I'm sorry, Brad. I just can't do this. I want more from a relationship than you can give.

Him: Oh, Tess. You've made me realize you're the only woman in the world for me. I'd be lost without you. (He drops to one knee and whips out a Tiffany ring box. Flicking it open, the diamond blinds me for a moment.) Marry me, Tess. Be mine forever.

Me: Put that 1.2 million dollar ring back in your pocket. We're not meant to be to be together. I must go.

Him: Wait! Tess! (He bursts into racking sobs.)

Me: (I wipe a tear as I head for the subway. My posture is excellent.)

Nice, huh? Okay, so here's what really happened.

Me: I don't think we can, I mean, uh, I don't think I

can see you anymore."

Him: Okay.

Me: (pulling the knife from the center of my heart) Bye.

The first one's better. MUCH better, don't you think? Unfortunately, Brad, bless his pointed little head, didn't understand that he was losing a gem. That I am, indeed, one hell of a catch and he's a fool for letting me go.

Really. I meant that. Honest.

I love it, Erin, that you've been so lucky with your Man To Do. And I really mean that, too. I sit here and wonder where I went wrong. Dating dangerous, fabulously wealthy, terminally handsome boys seemed like a good idea at the time. What was a broken heart (or ten)? Nevertheless, I've learned my lesson. No more Men To Do... I'm doing Men To Marry now. Period. The end. Well, not the end so much as the beginning. A new beginning with a whole new me.

I'm going to do all the things Dear Abby suggests: church socials (note to self: find church), night classes (note to self: ditto), afternoon concerts in Central Park, maybe some golf lessons. I am determined to find Mr. Right and become Mrs. Right by the end of the year. Or next year. Soon, okay? So no more Brads. Ever!

So don't you guys worry about me. Don't give your poor, desperate friend a second thought. I mean it.

Okay then. I'll just go cry myself to sleep. TTYS

Love and kisses

Tess

HARLEQUIN *Blaze*™

From:	Erin Thatcher
To:	Samantha Tyler; Tess Norton
Subject:	Men To Do

Men to do!

Ladies, I'm talking about a hot fling with the type of man no girl in her right mind would settle down with. You know, a man to *do* before we say "I do." What do you think? Couldn't we use an uncomplicated sexfest? Why let men corner the market on fun when we girls have the same urges and needs? I've already picked mine out....

Don't miss the steamy new Men To Do miniseries from bestselling Blaze authors!

THE SWEETEST TABOO by Alison Kent
December 2002

A DASH OF TEMPTATION by Jo Leigh
January 2003

A TASTE OF FANTASY by Isabel Sharpe
February 2003

Available wherever Harlequin books are sold.

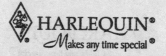

HARLEQUIN®
Makes any time special ®

There's something for everyone...

Behind the
Red Doors

From favorite authors

Vicki Lewis Thompson

Stephanie Bond

Leslie Kelly

A fun and sexy collection about the romantic encounters
that take place at The Red Doors lingerie shop.

**Behind the Red Doors—
you'll never guess which one leads to love...**

Look for it in January 2003.

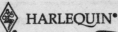

magazine

♥─────────────────────── **quizzes**

Is he the one? What kind of lover are you? Visit the **Quizzes** area to find out!

♥─────────────── **recipes for romance**

Get scrumptious meal ideas with our **Recipes for Romance**.

♥─────────────── **romantic movies**

Peek at the **Romantic Movies** area to find Top 10 Flicks about First Love, ten Supersexy Movies, and more.

♥─────────────────── **royal romance**

Get the latest scoop on your favorite royals in **Royal Romance**.

♥─────────────────────── **games**

Check out the **Games** pages to find a ton of interactive romantic fun!

♥─────────────── **romantic travel**

In need of a romantic rendezvous? Visit the **Romantic Travel** section for articles and guides.

♥─────────────────── **lovescopes**

Are you two compatible? Click your way to the **Lovescopes** area to find out now!

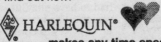

HARLEQUIN®

makes any time special—online...

Visit us online at
www.eHarlequin.com

COOPER'S CORNER

Welcome to Twin Oaks—
the new B and B in Cooper's Corner.
Some come for pleasure, others for
passion—and one to set things straight...

Coming in January 2003...
ACCIDENTAL FAMILY
by Kristin Gabriel

Check-in: When former TV soap star Rowena Dahl's biological clock started ticking, she opted to get pregnant at a fertility clinic. Unfortunately, she got the wrong sperm!

Checkout: Publisher Alan Rand was outraged that a daytime diva was having *his* baby. But he soon realized that he wanted Rowena as much as he wanted their child.

HARLEQUIN®
Makes any time special®